KANSAS, BLOODY KANSAS

The Missouri raiders were bleeding Kansas dry. Between them and their crazy dreams of conquest stood Lee Fisher, posing as one of the bloodthirsty crew with Emma Wright playing the part of his mistress. But before the debts' death calls were settled, Fisher and Emma got spilled into the wide-open game . . . a game that had only one prize: destruction.

Books by J. B. Dancer
in the Linford Western Library:

EVIL BREED
KANSAS, BLOODY KANSAS

J. B. DANCER

KANSAS, BLOODY KANSAS

Complete and Unabridged

99205

LINFORD
Leicester

F
D 22 ka

First Linford Edition
published August 1989

British Library CIP Data

Dancer, J. B.
  Kansas, bloody Kansas.—Large print ed.—
Linford western library
  Rn: John Harvey and Angus Wells   I. Title
823'. 914[F]

ISBN 0-7089-6720-5

Published by
F. A. Thorpe (Publishing) Ltd.
Anstey, Leicestershire
Set by Rowland Phototypesetting Ltd.
Bury St. Edmunds, Suffolk
Printed and bound in Great Britain by
T. J. Press (Padstow) Ltd., Padstow, Cornwall

1

SMOKE, thick and oily, filled the room. It clogged the man's lungs, burned at his throat, its pungency bringing tears to his eyes. The tears mingled with those already running down his bloodied cheeks, coursing through the grime, dribbling over the ragged flesh of his lips, through the crimson welling from his shattered nose.

He dragged himself crab-like over the rough planks, ignoring the splinters that studded his palms with the same forsaken indifference with which he ignored the embers sparking bright from the burning roof. He had only one thought in his mind: to reach Emily.

It didn't occur to him that Emily was dead.

No more than it occurred to him to save his life before the cabin fell in around him.

He climbed up on one knee, hauling his other leg behind him. It was broken just below the hip, where a scattergun had blasted its full load of buckshot through the worn cloth of his pants, his flesh and the bone beneath. He paid

1

no attention to the pain. He wanted only to reach his wife.

He had wanted to reach her since the raiders first kicked their way into the cabin. Had tried. But the shotgun stopped him. That and the boots pounding into his face and ribs. There had been a time of blackness after that, a time interrupted by the screaming of his wife as the men took her, one by one. Laughing. He had reached for the Colt Dragoon hung from its peg above the mantelshelf, counting a bullet for each man in the room. Then someone had lifted the gun in its old, wrinkled holster and swung it hard against his face. He had felt his nose break before the darkness closed in again and the pain came back.

The next time he opened his eyes the men were leaving.

Emily lay half-naked over the settle he had built, up against the far wall. Her dress was torn and her legs were spread wide. There was blood on her face and more on the floor.

He had begun to crawl when the first torch came in through the window. He cursed: the glass had cost him a deal of money in Lawrence, and a whole lot of sweat shipping it back on the wagon. The tar-coated brand spread flame over

2

the rough planks and he had slapped at them until his hands burned and the flickers went out. Then two more had come through, the second window broke and a rain of torches showered in. Then he had ignored them, dragging himself through the flames towards Emily.

It was hard going. One of the raiders had tramped his left hand to a bloody pulp and he thought his other wrist was cracked. He knew that his ribs were busted and threatening to poke up into his lungs.

But he kept on going.

After a while that felt a whole lot longer he realised the cabin was burning. The walls and roof were aflame, sparks flaming down over his head and back.

He paid the pain no heed.

Emily . . .

Must reach Emily.

Tend her. Comfort her. Tell her it was all right.

He reached the sprawled body of his wife as the roof caved in.

It was built of honest Kansas timber, dried out by the Kansas sun and the eternal wind. It was tinder dry and ready to burn.

It came down over him like hailstones falling from hell. Hot, agonising, burning.

He screamed, feeling the fire cascade over his body. He sucked in a breath and felt fire sear his lungs. He tried to scream again, but his lips blackened and blistered, his hair took flame and his eyes scorched.

The last thing he saw was Emily's burning hair, red flame on auburn as her face blackened and the world grew red.

Outside the cabin the Jayhawkers laughed.

There were seven of them. Six had gone in, one had held the horses, nervous at the sudden gush of flame that erupted from the cabin.

They watched as a man's life fell around him. Laughed as he died. Laughed at what they had done to his wife, the joke made greater by his helpless presence.

When the cabin was a smouldering ruin of fallen timber and sparking ash they rode away, slapping grimy hips in amusement, cheering one another on.

They rode fast, eager to reach the banks of the Kansas river and follow the waterway on eastwards to the safety of Missouri.

They were ugly-looking men with the ash

4

from the cabin griming their faces and their clothes, smearing over the blood that speckled their rag-tag attempts at a uniform. Most wore the heavy-woven pants of a farmer, and their jackets were a mixture of home-made cloth and the upper part of store-bought suits. Their unification came from the dark-dyed shirts they wore: sombre red, almost maroon, and stitched with hand-sewn designs.

They wore solid-looking gunbelts that carried a brace of pistols each, extra guns holstered on their saddles. A few bore single-shot rifles—Spencers or Henrys—and they all carried long, evil-looking knives in sheaths belted to waist or saddle.

Their leader, the big, dark man who rode at the head of the ragged column, carried a Meteor shotgun cradled in his right arm.

A thick spread of beard shaded his lower face, but above the hair glinted cold blue eyes that scanned the ground ahead with the flickering gaze of a snake. He wore two .44 Colt's Dragoon pistols on his belt. The left-hand gun was holstered with the butt forwards; the right was hung in the usual fashion. He carried a Spencer carbine on his saddle and a satisfied grin on his face.

He lifted his left hand as they came to the river.

"Easy now, boys." His voice was thick, slurred with the accents of the Missouri country. "Might be there's some nigger-lovers waitin' fer us. Let's bide a while an' test the water."

"Jesus, Caleb!" whined a voice from behind. "Let's get the hell back home. Afore the Redlegs raise up a posse."

"You scared, Jubal?"

The question was heavy with contempt.

"Hell, no," Jubal mumbled. "You know I ain't. I just don't figger it a good idea to wait around."

"Don't figger nuthin'," grunted the dark man. "You leave that to me."

Jubal opened his mouth to complain, but thought better of it. He looked away from the big man with the shotgun and found something on his saddle to occupy his attention. His lips moved silently, but he took care that no-one should see the curses he mouthed.

"Vinny, Jace." Two men urged their mounts forwards. "You go check it out. Hold to the brush an' don't get seen. If it's clear, give a whistle."

The riders nodded and eased off into the trees. In moments they were hidden amongst the birches, shadow on shadow, moving silently through the sun-dappled woodland.

The others waited. There was no sign of pursuit, nor any sounds that might suggest ambush, but they remained alert, tensed, eyes and ears checking the surrounding terrain. After a while a jay shrieked its raucous cry, closely followed by another. Caleb heeled his horse into the trees, leading the column towards the river.

Vinny and Jace sat their animals on the river bank, slumped casually in the saddle.

"Ain't a soul around, Caleb. She's quieter 'n a whorehouse on Monday."

"Good. Let's get on over."

Caleb dismounted and walked his horse down the bank. A wide pathway had been dug out here, ending in a crude wooden jetty. Tied to the uprights was a solid-looking raft, twin drag ropes spanning out across the water. He led the pony on to the raft, murmuring encouragement as the animal felt the sway of the timbers beneath its hooves. There was room for three more animals before the raft was full, and the men took hold of the ropes, hauling the platform out into the current. The horses stayed calm, as though accustomed to the crossing, and the men brought the thing smoothly in to the far bank.

The raft was hauled back and the three remaining men went on board. Just to prove he wasn't scared, Jubal insisted on being last. Cabel watched impassively, making—to the annoyance of the smaller man—no comment on this act of hind-sighted bravery.

When they were regrouped on the north bank of the Smoky Hill Caleb nodded, turning his horse eastwards.

"Let's go. The Captain'll be waitin' to hear what happened."

It was night before they reached their destination, the township of Independence on the boundary between Kansas and Missouri. They split up there, each man heading for his home with the confidence of honest citizens. Or men sure of a sound alibi.

Caleb headed for a saloon.

The Lost Dog was crowded out with rivermen and cowboys, a sprinkling of farmers and the usual drifters who seemed to pass from one bottle to the next, moving on when the money ran out and the problem of work raised its unwelcome head. He shoved through the drinkers, ignoring several invitations to sit in on card games, and elbowed his way to the stairs.

He paused at the head, cold, black eyes scanning the room with innate caution, then turned to a door halfway along the balcony. Tapping once on the thin panelling, he waited until the man inside invited him to enter.

Once through the door he felt, as always, that he had stepped into another world. Thick carpets covered the floor, their richness muffling his footsteps; heavy drapes covered the windows, and a screen of lacquered wood formed a kind of portico beyond the door. The furniture was hand-carved from heavy, reddish-black mahogany. Paintings hung on the walls. The place was a far cry from anything Caleb had seen this side of St. Louis and he hated to think what it must have cost to ship the stuff in.

He doffed his hat, suddenly nervous as the man seated on the banquette stared at him.

"Well?" the voice was dry as a Kansas dust storm. And equally menacing. "How did it go?"

"Well," answered Caleb. "We killed Strother

an' his wife. Fired the cabin. By now there won't be but ashes."

"Excellent. Did anyone see you?"

"No. We rode in like we was on the way to a prayer meetin'. Same comin' out."

"The blacks? What about them?"

"Runnin' scared. They saw us comin' an' took off like their arses was on fire. Frank an' Vinny wanted to chase 'em, but I said not to."

"Quite right. They'll learn their lesson and come to heel. No point to destroying sound breeding stock. You did well, Caleb."

"Thanks, Captain."

Caleb grinned through his beard like a schoolboy praised for handling a lesson well. He waited until the other man motioned him to sit down, then curled his big frame into a leather armchair.

"Whisky?"

"Thanks, sir. I'd appreciate it."

The man reached out to the crystal decanter on the low table beside him and poured two glasses. Caleb took a long, grateful swallow and studied him over the rim.

He was thin as Caleb was broad, a sparse, skeletal man with bright, burning blue eyes set in deep-sunk sockets that seemed to carry a

10

permanent shadow about them. He was dressed in a tailored frock-coat of black linen, tight-fitting pants of the same material sitting snug over side-button boots polished so gleaming clean they reflected the light of the ornate lamp hung from the low ceiling. His shirt was of white lawn, frilled at cuff and collar, a cravat of burgundy silk fastened at the neck with a diamond pin.

The face was pale, a stranger to the sun, narrow lips set beneath a thin wedge of nose. The forehead was high, waxy in the yellow light, and his hair gleamed black and sleek as his footwear.

He had come to Independence a year ago with two wagon loads of furniture and a trunk stuffed full of money.

His name was Jonas Vickers. Captain Jonas Vickers. And he was mean as an angry diamondback.

He had taken up residence in the Lost Dog and command of Caleb's jayhawking gang. Two men had argued that takeover: both were dead. Vickers wore a .36 Colt's Navy in a shoulder rig and used the gun faster than any man Caleb had ever seen. Caleb James was lacking in education, but he was no fool. He had recognised a leader when he saw Vickers, and guessed that the cold, calm man would guide him to more money than he could make on his own. He had accepted Jonas Vickers without question.

So far it had proven a sound decision.

"So," murmured Vickers in that dust-dry voice, "we must plan our next move."

"Wilde must be feelin' the pinch by now," suggested Caleb. "I'd think he's contemplatin' a get-out."

Vickers shook his head, helping himself to more whisky.

"You don't know Robert Wilde like I do, Caleb. He's not a man to quit easily."

"Hell!" Caleb emptied his glass and waited to be offered more. "We burned out seven o' his tenants. We run off more o' his niggers than he can afford. How can he keep goin'?"

"Diversions," grated Vickers, "minor skirmishes to test his strength. What we must do now is hit him hard. Hit him in the heart."

"What?" Caleb sounded almost frightened. "Raid Northville? We don't have the men for it."

"We can get them," said Vickers evenly, "it's just a question of timing it right. Things are hotting up, my friend. Like a kettle on the stove, the South is boiling over. There'll be war before long. Take my word on it. If things go on as they are now the South will secede and draw the damn' yankees into civil war. And war, Caleb, can make men rich."

"Yeah," grunted Caleb, out of his depth. "I'll go along with that. I got no time fer nigger-lovers an' less fer yankees, but I still can't see us raidin' Northville. The place is too damn' strong. Wilde owns the town."

"Towns can change hands, Caleb." Vickers' voice was softer now, almost pleasant as he relished his private thoughts. "Just as power does. And with Northville under our control we shall hold a great deal of power."

It was a warm summer that year of 1856, and tempers matched the heat.

In May, United States Marshal J. B. Donaldson had led a posse of eight hundred men into Lawrence, Kansas, to quell potential anti-slavery riots. The posse became a mob: two newspaper offices, a hotel, and the governor's home were burned to the ground.

In the Senate, Congressman Preston Brooks of South Carolina beat Charles Sumner of Massachusetts to a bloody pulp. He used a cane, and during the following weeks jubilant Southerners showered the six-foot Congressman with presentation canes.

The new telegraph system brought the news to Kansas. On 24th May it reached a fervent anti-slavery supporter called John Brown. Brown led eight men, four of them his own sons, to Pottawatomie Creek. Systematically, Brown's vigilantes butchered five homesteaders.

In Washington, dissatisfied Northerners flocked to the support of the new-formed Republican party, pushing John Charles Fremont forwards as their candidate for the presidential seat. The South allied itself behind James Buchanan of the Democratic party, and saw him elected to the White House.

And a gangling, earnest man, a lawyer from the Northwest frontier country fought hard to preserve the rights of all men, black or white. He was tall and ugly. His name was Abraham Lincoln.

The heat of summer baked Kansas.

And feelings ran higher than the temperature.

Fanatics like John Brown pursued a course of bloody massacre in support of their cause. Southern sympathisers answered in equal measure. Kansas redlegs fought Missouri jayhawkers. Half the people of Kansas turned to the North, the other half set their eyes to Richmond, in the South. And cut-throat gangs rode in to make the best of the rich pickings set out like appetisers for the coming war.

Kansas earned its nickname: Kansas, Bloody Kansas.

2

THE cigar smoke was beginning to bother Lee Fisher.

It filled the rosewood-panelled office with a thick fug of aromatic blue mist that stung his nostrils and watered his eyes enough to make him blink. Fisher didn't enjoy discomfort. He could put up with it. Had, more often than not.

But he didn't enjoy it.

He stood up and moved over to the window.

"Go ahead, open it."

The speaker was a big, ruddy-faced man in an expensive suit cut to hide the spread of his stomach. He waved his cigar as he turned to glance at Fisher, reminding the younger man who was the boss.

"Thanks."

Fisher's voice was faintly accented, a mixture of French-Canadian and pure American with an overlay of the guttural throat sounds the Indians use. It was not surprising: he was born in the Northwest, on the high branch of the Missouri,

16

where his parents had died. After that he had lived with the Blackfeet, become an Indian. It was something ingrained, a part of him, even though he now wore a fashionable black suit complete with silver watch-chain spread across his lean ribs and a rakish moustache that made him look older than his natural span of twenty-seven years.

"Don't mention it. And try not to sound so damn' surly. I can't help it if you don't like my cigars."

Albert C. Wilder grinned as Fisher turned away, staring out at the bustle of the St. Louis streets, and leaned forwards across the wide, leather-topped desk to stab his huge cigar at Bradford McGarry.

"You follow me so far, Brad?"

McGarry nodded, sparking light off the thin gold frames of his owlish spectacles. "Sure, though I'd like to hear some more."

He was older than Fisher, and a good deal heavier, a short, compact man with the bland face and mouse-brown hair of a book-keeper or hotel clerk. Where Fisher was dark, McGarry was pale: in face, hair, even manner. His suit lacked the dash of Fisher's and his manner was almost apologetic. It belied the mind. It served him well as an undercover agent for Wilder's detection and protection agency.

If Fisher was the cold steel, then McGarry was the subtle poison. They made a good team, had done before. The two men and the woman seated beside the brown man.

Emma Wright was twenty-three and beautiful. The demure dress she wore was impeccably cut, but could no more hide her curves than a wet sheet. Its rich green accented the auburn of her long hair, complementing the green of her eyes and the full lusciousness of her mouth.

Fisher turned back from the window, grinning at her.

She ignored him studiously, which afforded him more amusement. One day, he promised himself, you'll look me in the eye and say "please". One day.

Lee Fisher was good with women. Almost as good as he was with a gun. But Emma refused to know, had even threatened him once with the little gun she carried. That thought made Lee Fisher smile again as he recalled where she holstered the tiny Remington-Elliot derringer. It was almost worth risking a bullet to see that smooth spread of soft-fleshed thigh.

He pushed the memory from his mind, concentrating on Wilder as he walked back into the heavy smoke.

"All right," said the big man, "let's run over it again, just in case Lee, here, got his mind mixed up in a petticoat.

"You three did real good bringing the Stillwell gang in, but this new one sounds like something different. Something a whole lot harder."

He dropped his cigar into an ashtray that was already threatening to overwhelm the desk and reached for a fresh cylinder of dark tobacco.

"Kansas is in one hell of a mess. There's Southern sympathisers raiding out of Missouri and Kansas vigilantes answering back. The territory looks set for its own private war, which won't have a whole lot to do with the big one I think is coming. It's natural breeding ground for outlaws. Like a pond is for mosquitoes. There's one particular gang that's giving more trouble than its worth: all we know about it is that folks call it the Captain's Band and it's been hitting a big landowner called Robert Wilde."

He snipped the end from his cigar with a

19

practised movement and waited as McGarry held a lit match to the tip.

"Wilde is getting worried. Thinks there's someone masterminding a plan to drive him out. He wants us to find out who. And stop them."

"And that's all?" Fisher asked. "We don't know anything more?"

"No." Wilder shook his head. "Except that Wilde has his headquarters in a place called Northville, just south of the Smoky Hill river. He thinks the raiders are mostly from Missouri. Probably a town on the border, somewhere like Independence. It's as good a place as any to start."

"Start what?" asked Fisher. "What do we do? Ride in and begin asking questions?"

Brad McGarry shrugged and Emma shot him a withering glance. Wilder contented himself with a long puff of smoke that ended up curling its way about Fisher's face.

"No, Lee," he said patiently. "You're not trapping now, nor hunting runaway gunmen. You're working for me, and you'll do that quieter and smoother. Settle down and listen."

Fisher grinned. He enjoyed needling his

employer almost as much as he enjoyed needling Brad.

"I thought out a plan," said the big man.
"Brad here goes direct to Northville. Wilde
reckons the outlaws might hit at him, so he
wants a bodyguard." McGarry nodded. "You,
Lee, head for Independence. The way you look
and that fancy accent, you might come from the
South. That's your cover, anyway. You just sit
in there and keep your ears open."

"What about me?" Emma sounded irritable,
as though she felt left out of things. "What do
I do?"

"That's easy," said Wilder. "You go along
with Lee. You play the part of his mistress. A
southern belle following her man."

Fisher let a slow whistle shrill from his lips.

"Now that," he said, "is the kind of cover I
like."

Emma glared at him, her green eyes blazing.

"It's just a cover. Nothing more. Don't start
getting ideas."

"Beds got covers," grinned Fisher, "and if
you're supposed to be sleeping with me, we
can't book separate rooms."

McGarry glanced at Emma. "I don't like it.

Why not send Lee to Northville? I can go along with Emma."

Wilder chuckled, spilling ash over his vest. "Wouldn't work, Brad. Lee's the one to pass for a Southerner, not you. No, it's the way I told you. No other."

Fisher grinned as he crossed the room. Leaning over Emma, he rested his hands on her shoulders, ignoring Brad's angry stare.

"Well, Emma," he murmured, "shall we go practise our cover story?"

Fisher and Emma reached Independence eleven days later. They had travelled by riverboat up the Missouri, sharing a cabin in a spiky kind of partnership that left Lee stretched nightly on the narrow seat of the uncomfortable sofa built into their stateroom. By the time they reached their destination he was irritable and aching; Emma was irritable and well-rested and slept with a derringer under her pillow. Five times the little gun had levelled on Fisher, driving him back to the cold comfort of his lonely bed.

Bradford McGarry travelled on a separate boat, leaving it at Independence two days before the others arrived to ride overland to Northville.

He didn't like this assignment. Liked even less the way Lee had turned up to wish him a good journey. "Maybe you'll find some company on the boat," the tall man had said, "as enjoyable as mine."

McGarry had refused to rise to the bait. He was aware of Fisher's way with women, recognised that the dark man was attractive, if too flashy for his own taste. Knew, too, that Fisher thought him dull and plodding. overly concerned with formalities and the good name of the Agency. In turn, McGarry thought Fisher too careless of the responsibilities he had assumed on joining the organisation, too ready to bend the unspoken rules.

He remembered an argument they had got into days before. McGarry had maintained that to stay safe—alive—it was necessary to work by the book, that certain rules existed governing their actions. Fisher had laughed. "Sure there's a book we go by," he had grinned. "But mine's only got one rule in it: stay alive. Any damn' way you can."

McGarry had left it. There was little point in arguing with Lee: he was too damn' confident. In every way.

But the thought of him and Emma sharing a

cabin still brought an angry flush to McGarry's face and he had hidden his irritation behind a frown as he walked up the gangplank. Dammit to hell! The Chief could have sent Lee to Northville and him to Missouri. That way he might have made some headway with Emma.

He shook his head, forcing the troublesome thoughts from his mind. Worrying about Emma and Lee would do him no good, and from what the Chief had said about the set-up, he would need his full concentration to settle this assignment successfully.

He rode on through the wooded country flanking the river, following the Kansas river west towards Lawrence. When he spotted the town he turned south through the pine breaks, preferring to stay away from people until he made contact with Wilde.

That night he camped out beneath the overhang of a bluff, using the rocks to shade his fire. Around midnight he heard a group of horsemen go by somewhere below him.

They were too far away to be anything more than a clatter of sound, and so he let them pass, waiting until the hoofbeats faded away in the distance before settling down to sleep.

The next morning he found out where they were headed.

There was a cabin built in a small clearing, the stumps of dead trees showing where the homesteader had cleared the ground. It was very quiet and no smoke showed from the stack forming the end wall of the place. McGarry reined in on the edge of the pines and called a greeting.

There was no answer.

He eased his long-barrelled Mississippi rifle from the saddle scabbard and thumbed the hammer back. Then he dismounted and went forwards on foot.

The door of the cabin hung open, a thick cluster of flies buzzing around the frame. McGarry circled the place, keeping to the shadow of the big trees. Behind the place was a rough corral. It contained four dead pigs. He moved on, swinging closer until he was up against the side wall. There were shutters down over the windows and he had to sidle on to the door before he could see inside.

The rifle led the way in, McGarry jumping through the flies as he dropped to a crouch, eyes scanning the gloomy interior.

He gagged on the stink, flapping a hand

about his face to drive off the furious, buzzing insects.

Three bodies lay inside the cabin; one was white, the others black. All were very dead. Shot at close range with heavy calibre guns. Shot more than was necessary to kill a man. Shot in rage or hate, so that faces and bodies were pulped and broken.

McGarry held his breath until he was a good distance from the cabin, then let it out in a long sigh of disgust. Killing was a necessary part of his job, he accepted that; could kill fast himself when the situation demanded. Mutilation was something else. Bradford McGarry had little sympathy with that kind of killing.

He climbed back on his horse and turned south again.

Around noon, he reached Northville. It was a small town by Eastern standards, large for an open territory like Kansas. On two sides the hills surrounded the place, the breaks giving way to open plain that was mostly yellow with wheat and high-standing corn. The town looked prosperous. It had a wide central street with secondary tracks leading off at right angles. He used his telescope to check the place out: Wilder had given him a brief description, but

McGarry was a naturally careful man who preferred to make his own judgments.

There was one hotel, a flat-roofed, single-storey place, and a scattering of stores. A stable was located at one end of the main street and cattle pens at the other. High-standing wind-mills turned lazily in the faint breeze, pumping water into catchment tanks built up alongside. There was one saloon and a thin spread of single-level houses; a church completed the picture of quiet success.

McGarry folded the eye-glass and stowed it back in his saddlebag. Wilde had an office next to the hotel. He headed for it.

The town was quiet, and when he reached Wilde's office there was a sign hung behind the glass, the hand-lettering announcing its closure until three. McGarry walked his horse up the street to the stable, flipped the ostler a dollar, and asked where he could find Robert Wilde.

"Mister Wilde? He'll be takin' a meal down at the Phoenix House. Right next to his place."

"Thanks." McGarry draped his saddlebags over his shoulder, hefted the rifle in his left hand, and set off down the street.

The Phoenix House was trying hard to look like a plush St. Louis hotel. It was difficult with

Kansas dust in the air and the red velvet of the upholstery was faded, the carpets grimed with dirt and the markings of high-heeled boots. A clerk pointed out Wilde, and McGarry took time to study the man.

He was big, muscle beginning to turn flabby, and grey showed in his reddish hair. His eyes, though, remained bright, and McGarry noticed that the dark jacket was turned back over the butt of a Colt's Dragoon. He was spooning stew into his mouth, spilling it on his moustache without bothering to wipe it away.

McGarry crossed the room. "Mr. Wilde? I'm Bradford McGarry."

"Jesus Christ!" Wilde waved his left hand, gesturing the agent to sit down. "I'm glad you've come."

As McGarry introduced himself to Wilde, Lee Fisher and Emma Wright were settling into the Creole Palace in Independence.

Fisher handed the Negro porter a fifty cent tip and waved away the man's thanks, herding him out of the room as Emma turned towards him.

"You're too free with that money," she said accusingly. "Our expenses aren't limitless."

"Sweetheart," grinned Fisher lazily, "if I'm risking my life for a man who can't handle his own trouble, I expect him to pay for the privilege. Anyways, I'm a Southern gentleman, remember."

"Don't call me sweetheart," snapped Emma. "I don't like it."

Fisher shrugged, the lazy smile still playing over his handsome features.

"What should I call you? We're lovers, aren't we? I like the idea myself."

"You showed that on the river." Emma opened her clutch bag, lifting out the Remington-Elliot as a reminder. "Don't start getting ideas again."

Lee watched her as she checked the tiny .22 pistol, then flipped his hat on to the wide bed.

"You plannin' to check the other one?" he asked innocently. "Might be as well."

Emma blushed. "No need. It's working well enough to stop you."

"Maybe," said Fisher. "And then, maybe not. We should find out someday."

Emma snorted, turning away to look over their rooms. She was grateful that their cover demanded a lavish outlay of money—conscious as she was of following Wilder's standard dictum about holding expenses to a moderate level, she was grateful that they were located in a suite rather than the usual single-room. The bed, she decided, would be hers; Lee could sleep comfortably on the divan in the salon. And there was a door between the rooms. Better still, there was a lock on the door. She eased the key loose with practised skill, palming it as she sauntered back to drop it into her bag.

Fisher didn't notice. He was intent on the street below, checking the windows of the buildings opposite, watching the passers-by as though he hoped to pick the outlaws of the Captain's Band from the crowds of innocent citizens.

"Let's go eat," he said abruptly. "I'm too hungry to try anything on a fire-eater like you right now."

Curiously, when Emma saw him eyeing their waitress she felt vaguely irritated, as though resentful that he should pay attention to other women. The fact that she felt irritated made her angry with herself and she concentrated on her food, hiding her confusion behind a mask of hunger.

"Well, sweetheart." Lee ignored the dainty

30

foot that slammed into his ankle. "What shall we do now? You fancy a stroll around?"

Emma nodded. "Why not? Honey."

The way she said it made the word an insult. Fisher just smiled and rose to his feet. Decorously, he walked around the table to hold her chair as she stood up, extending his left arm for her to hold as he escorted her out of the restaurant.

A negro servant opened the big doors and they stepped out into bright sunlight, pausing under the shade of the porch as they glanced right and left along the street.

"Let's take a walk," murmured Fisher, "and check this place out. We'd best find a stable and hire us some horses. We might be needing them."

"We're Southern gentlefolk," answered Emma with a false smile. "Remember? We use carriages."

"Sure," grinned Fisher. "We'll hire a carriage, too. I just feel like knowing there's a pony around if I want to get out fast."

Emma gave in to the sense of the argument and made up her mind to be—at least—polite. There wasn't really any other way to play it. And when Lee wasn't being too pushy he could be pleasant company. That was something she had to admit. Even if she didn't like to.

She kept quiet and studied the town.

Independence was smaller than St. Louis. Inevitably, as the only communication with the prosperous eastern lands came via the river or the overland trails. Direct communication, that was. The telegraph wires had pushed far enough west to keep the town informed of events in the capital cities, and express riders or the Butterfield stage brought mail packets in.

But it was ready access of materials and men that determined a town's growth, and Independence was still waiting for the promised railroad to push its slow way west before any real growth could begin. The lines were now some thirteen or fourteen miles out from St. Louis, the gangers waiting for the politicians and the businessmen to end their wrangling and devote the necessary finances to the grand policy of westward expansion before the real push could begin.

Even so, Independence was wealthy.

Situated on the confluence of the Missouri and the Kansas rivers, the town had access to both the wheat and cattle lands of the west and south, and a link with the east. The Oregon

Trail began there, winding north and west into Nebraska and Wyoming, up into the Montana Territory and the high peaks of the Great Divide. The California Trail looped off from the Oregon, and the old route to Santa Fe linked the town with the rich Mexican possessions.

Independence benefited from its siting. It had about it an air of prosperity, of bustle and business. And of tension.

Slaves eased unobtrusively through the crowds, darting past horsemen and wagons, stepping aside to make room on the wide boardwalks for the white citizens. Swarthy, loud-voiced rivermen rubbed shoulders with cowboys and farmers. Housewives and whores ignored one another with equal disdain. Frock-coated businessmen jostled with shirt-sleeved labourers, and here and there showed a hand-stitched shirt of dark maroon, patterned with yellow or white embroidery.

The one thing most men had in common, Fisher noticed, was their armament. Guns were natural: west of the Mississippi a man without a gun was some kind of freak. But here there seemed to be more. He noticed that those gentlemen who did not wear a gun on their waist had a tell-tale bulge under their jackets. And the majority carried two pistols, slung in worn holsters from either hip.

And few let their hands stray far from the butts.

Lee Fisher had little interest in the political tensions afflicting the mid-Western territories. He was too used to the exigencies of life in the Northwest. Montana, the Dakota Territory, Wyoming, Nebraska; a man wore a gun there because if he didn't some Indian, a Sioux or a Cheyenne, a Blackfoot or a Crow, Shoshoni or Pawnee, would take his horses and maybe his life. Negroes, up there, were as strange as the growing conflict between North and South, the arguments of industry against cotton.

It was a thing he had never thought about. A Negro was one more man, friend or enemy in accordance with his feelings, but little different to anyone else. A few shades darker than an Indian, not much darker than the French-Canadian trappers he had known as a boy. The Blackfeet who raised him after killing his mother had owned slaves; captured Sioux, some Crow women; they were a natural part of the tribe's life. Slaves won in battle were accepted as normal, became a part of the tribe.

But here it seemed that the whites regarded the blacks as naturally inferior, without the right of honourable conquest. And more disturbing still, the Negroes seemed to agree.

He wondered why he had not noticed it in St. Louis. Perhaps because there it was an accepted form of life, the slave owners treating their possessions with a degree of respect: like a rancher taking care of a cow or a horse, wary of wasting valuable property.

He decided to ask about the situation before opting for one side or the other; for now he had a clear assignment, and so long as that lasted, he would work for Wilde—for the anti-slavery faction, if that was how it got defined.

"You're suddenly quiet."

Emma's voice interrupted his musings.

"I'm sorry." He grinned at her. "I guess I should be paying more attention to my mistress."

"Dammit," said Emma, unladylike. "Do you have to misunderstand everything I say?"

"No," he smiled. "I just prefer it that way."

Emma looked angry until he reminded her of their cover story, then fixed a sweet smile on her pretty face, biting off her anger.

They found a stable and hired a two-in-hand

rig that looked fitting for a Southern gentleman and his lady. Fisher drove the little buggy out with casual skill, steering the high-stepping horses up the street until he was out of sight of the stable.

For a two cent tip a Negro guided them to a second ostlery, and Fisher hitched his rig alongside the adjoining building, walking on to the stable.

It was a run-down looking place, but the horses inside were sound, well-fed and carefully tended. He hired two, a tall black stallion that took his fancy, and a smaller dun gelding. He handed over thirty dollars for an indefinite period, saddlery thrown in, then passed over twenty dollars more for the stablehand to keep his mouth shut.

Satisfied, he walked back to Emma and explained the arrangement.

The woman studied him with new respect. "Perhaps you're not so careless as I thought. That's the first sensible thing you've done so far."

Fisher smiled cheerfully. "You changing your mind about me? Maybe there's hope yet."

He whipped the horses up to a canter before

she could answer, grinning as she shrieked and grabbed at his arm to keep her balance.

They spent the afternoon exploring the town and by the time they got back to the hotel both agents were confident of the lay-out. Fisher tipped a porter to drive the rig back to the stable and escorted Emma with all due respect up to their room.

A bathroom had been built into a corner of the suite, off from the bedchamber, and Emma called for hot water. To Lee's annoyance she locked the adjoining door before sinking into the tub. When she emerged it was as a full-blown southern belle. Her hair was piled up in a cascade of auburn ringlets, artfully teased over pale shoulders set off by the rich purple of her low-cut dress. She carried a fan and a tiny, pearl-woven bag. Her make-up was discreetly applied to come out just the wrong side of proper. The enticing side.

Fisher bowed his approval.

"Why, ma'am," he grinned, "I do assure you, you look purely lovely."

"Go take a bath," said Emma. "Then we can find out who's who in this town."

Fisher took her hand. Kissed it decorously. And went off to take a bath as ordered.

3

THE Glory Hole saloon was packed out when Lee Fisher pushed in through the batwing doors. A few men turned to glance up at him, but then their attention was drawn back to the man standing on a table at the far end of the long room.

Fisher skirted round the crowd, fetching up against the bar where he called for whisky. He listened to the speaker as the bartender pushed a glass and a bottle of pale-looking liquor over in his direction. For a saloon mob, they were surprisingly quiet, paying full attention to the words of the skinny, bright-eyed man addressing them.

It was mostly about slavery, with a distinct bias towards the abolishment side of the argument. The bulk of the crowd seemed to be in agreement, but there was a cluster of men off to one side of the saloon who obviously held different views.

Fisher waited, watching to see what happened.

It wasn't long coming. The speaker was shouting something about the dignity of mankind when a bottle caught him along the side of his head, sending him staggering off the table. A trio of boatmen caught him before he hit the floor, shoving him unceremoniously back on the table as they waded into the flaring fight.

Someone had swung a punch at the bottle thrower. Felt it answered by the wrong end of a billy-club. Then a full-scale saloon brawl was in progress.

Fisher leaned back on the bar, nursing his drink. Watching as an idea began to take shape.

"Christ, mister! You want to get stomped on?"

The bartender tugged at his sleeve.

"I can look after myself," answered Fisher. "Why'd they do that, anyway? Looks to me like they're a long way outnumbered here."

"You better believe it." The barkeep pulled a sawed-off shotgun into view as he spoke. "Most folks as come in here tend to side with the North. Them boys that threw the bottle, they're good ole Southern boys. Don't take kindly to that free-the-nigger talk."

39

"How about you?" Fisher asked. "Which side you come down on?"

"Mister," grunted the bartender, "the only side I'm on is this one. Right here behind the bar. So long as a man's got money fer his likker, I ain't got no side."

"Good," said Fisher. "In that case you won't be needing that scattergun."

He reached over as he said it, folding his left hand into the man's shirt front to drag him forwards, his right closing over the stubby barrels of the ugly weapon. He twisted the shotgun out of the man's grasp and released his grip on the dirty collar. The barkeep stared in amazement as he checked the load and moved towards the mob.

"You're crazy! They'll take you apart."

"I doubt it," called Fisher. "You ever see a sober man go up against a scattergun when he had some kind of choice?"

The barman was too busy climbing under the counter to answer. Fisher snapped the shotgun closed and thumbed back the left side hammer. Pointing the barrel at the ceiling he squeezed the trigger.

There was a sound like rolling thunder and a shower of splinters from the roof. Several men yelped as pellets ricocheted over their faces, and the mob fell silent, turning towards Fisher.

He smiled. Cold. And thumbed back the second hammer.

"It won't take you all," he said pleasantly, "but it'll sure make a mess of some. Now why don't you back off them good old boys down there and give 'em room to move on out? Before I get tired of holding this hammer back."

The crowd stood for a moment, then the men at the front measured the width of the barrel and shuffled sideways. A path cleared through the mob, revealing a tight-knit group of bruised men with clubs and broken bottles in their hands.

"You boys care to step out?" grinned Fisher. "I don't reckon these gentlemen will do too much to stop you."

The group surged forwards, cutting through the crowd with grateful looks on their battered faces. Fisher moved after them, the scattergun held at waist height.

When he reached the doors he backed through and lowered the hammer. Tossing the gun aside, he ran up the street after the others. One man turned to wait for him.

"That was real welcome, friend." He was a

short, weaselly-looking man. "I guess you share our feelin's about nigger-lovers."

"Looks that way, don't it?" grunted Fisher. "I thought you could use some help."

"We sure needed it," agreed Weasel-face. "We never figgered them milk-belly bastards to take on so."

He tugged at Fisher's sleeve, drawing the tall man down a side street.

"Best we cut off here. They could come after us, but this way I can lose them. Where you stayin'?"

"The Creole Palace," answered Fisher, slowing his pace to accommodate the shorter man.

"Real nice. You new in town?"

"Got in today." Fisher heard the admiration in the man's voice: the Creole Palace had been a good choice. "Came up river from St. Louis."

"Yeah." Weasel-face nodded, as though pleased with himself for guessing right. "I had you figgered fer a riverboat man. That suit an' all. You a gambler?"

Fisher smiled, thinking of the long-shot he had only just taken. "Yeah, you could say that."

"Thought it'd be somethin' like that." The

man ducked into a dark alley, glancing up at Fisher. "Knew you was from the South when I heard your voice. I'm real smart on things like that."

Sure you are, thought Fisher, smart enough to talk your neck into a rope and congratulate yourself for getting the knot tight.

He said: "You make a habit of taking on the nigger-lovers?"

Weasel-face laughed. "Sure do. It's gotten to be kinda like mixin' business an' pleasure."

"How's that?" Fisher kept his voice deliberately casual: one Southern-sympathiser to another. "I didn't see too much business back there, nor so much pleasure."

"Shit, it ain't always like that. Times are we have us a real good time. Profitable, too."

"Yeah? Sounds interesting," prompted Fisher. "How d'you work it?"

The short man chuckled, steering his companion down a new alleyway. He tapped a finger to the side of his bulbous nose, winking obscenely.

"Might be you'll find out someday. Right now it's more'n my life's worth to tell."

"I damn' near saved your life," grunted

Fisher, pretending hurt. "I thought we was on the same side."

"Now don't go takin' offence." Weasel-face stopped in his tracks, turning to look up. "I'm real grateful fer that. Only it ain't fer me to go tellin' strangers about our doin's. You take my word on it, what we do is fer the South. Could be you'll get to learn about it. Right now you'll hafta wait."

"For what?" Fisher asked.

The little man was clearly enjoying the role of conspirator. He patted Fisher's arm in a consoling gesture and winked again, exposing blackened teeth in a leering smile.

"I need to talk to a few people. Real important people. Were it up to me, I'd let you in on it right now. Only it ain't just me." He preened like a ragged bantam. "There's others involved an' I gotta protect their interests. Don't you worry, though: you got my confidence an' I'm gonna tell 'em all about what you did. You just sit tight in that big ole hotel an' wait fer the word."

"Yeah, sure," said Fisher, hiding his amusement. "I'll do that."

The little man smiled, shuffling off into the darkness. Fisher followed him, guessing that

44

they were circling back towards main-street. He saw light ahead and halted as a greasy hand clutched again at his arm.

"I'm movin' on now," said Weasel-face, "an' you'd best forget you seen me. Just head on towards the lights, the Creole Palace is a block up, on yore left."

"Thanks," said Fisher, "what do I call you?"

"Jubal. Jubal Farrow. How 'bout you?"

"Fisher," he said. "Lee Fisher."

"Good to know you, Lee." Farrow stuck out a hand.

Fisher took it, doing his best to sound sincere. "Good to know you, Jubal. Maybe I'll be hearing from you."

"You bet. We can use men like you."

Farrow stepped back into the shadows and Lee heard the scrabble of boots on a fence, a grunt, then the weaselly man was gone into the night. He pulled a kerchief from his jacket and wiped his hand. It felt dirty. He tucked the cloth back in place and sauntered towards the hotel, thinking hard.

Jubal Farrow was obviously a pro-slavery man. From what he had said, he was most likely part of a gang. Whether that gang was the one threatening Wilde's outfit was something he

45

would have to wait to find out. At least he had established his credentials as a Southerner, a pro-slavery man.

Somewhat to his surprise, he found it left a sick feeling in his gut.

He reminded himself that he was here to do a job. A job that paid pretty well.

If making out that he had no time for Negroes was part of it, then that was a price that had to be paid. Like acting friendly with a slimy little gutter-crawler like Jubal Farrow.

Dammit, he told himself, you agreed to go through with it. Now go ahead and get it done.

He walked down to the end of the alley and turned off to the left, heading for the Creole Palace.

Emma was waiting for him in one of the side-rooms, sipping a sherry and looking angry. She turned as he came through the glass-pannelled doors, her green eyes sparking fire. He smiled apologetically and sat down beside her.

Emma smiled, leaning towards him so that her words should be muffled from the other guests.

"Where the devil have you been? You said you were going for a drink, not a round trip of Kansas. Do you realise I've been sitting here for two hours? I've fought off three men and the clerks are beginning to give me funny looks."

Fisher closed his hands over her white-gloved fist. It looked like a gesture of affection; he thought it a safe move to prevent her from slapping him.

"Sorry, honey. I got a little tied up. I beg your forgiveness."

He pitched his voice just loud enough to carry across the room, and leaned forwards to brush her cheek with his lips. His grip prevented Emma from pulling away. Across the room a grey-haired dowager smiled indulgently: the lovers were making up.

"Ham!" whispered Emma. "Where have you been?"

"I got in a fight." Lee gazed into her stormy green eyes. "It seemed like the best way to contact the people we're looking for. Getting back here took a while longer than I planned."

"What did you do?" snarled Emma from behind a smile. "Kill someone to prove you're on the right side?"

Lee felt hurt. "No. I happened in on a brawl. I think I saved the people we're looking for. At least, if not them, people who can introduce us."

47

"All right." Emma sounded slightly abashed. "Perhaps you did the right thing. Just try not to leave me alone again—there're too many men around here with an eye for a lone woman."

"Darling," said Fisher, "I'll defend your honour with my life."

He stood up before she could reply, crooking his elbow to accommodate her hand as he gestured towards the dining-room. Emma clamped her teeth over her instinctive comment and took his arm.

As they left the salon, they heard the grey-haired woman murmur something about love-birds.

Fisher grinned. Emma tried to drive her nails through his sleeve.

The restaurant was almost full, but their table was still held for them and a subservient *maître d'hôtel* ushered them to their places like visiting royalty. A jug of water and a pot of coffee were set on fancy stands at the centre of the table and a menu—printed, Fisher noticed in surprise—was handed to him. He ordered Missouri cray-fish and steaks, with fried potatoes and greens. Then the waiter in the stiff collar and black bow-tie arrived with the wine list. Fisher felt suddenly out of his depth.

48

No great drinking man at the best of times, he was accustomed to whisky and beer. Wine was something new, something he had tasted in St. Louis and enjoyed without ever getting used to it.

He was grateful when Emma came to his aid.

"Southern gentlemen." She emphasised the second word. "Know about wine. Tell the waiter to choose the best one. And for God's sake act like you know what you're doing."

More than a little embarrassed, Fisher took her advice. He also made a mental note to learn about wine. Drinking it would be the start of the lessons.

The food was good, and it went a long way to smoothing out their differences. Fisher took particular care to be polite, fighting down his natural dislike of having a woman for a partner. He had no real complaints about Emma, was attracted to her as much as he had ever been attracted to any woman, but he still didn't like the set-up. He felt that he could have done just as well—probably better—acting alone. A woman belonged at home. Cooking, raising kids, looking after her man; not out in the firing line of a potential war. When the shooting started in earnest he assumed he would have to find her a safe hiding place as the men got down to the real work.

Emma felt much the same, if from the opposite direction.

Lee Fisher, after all, was a very attractive man. Would be even more attractive if he could forget his prejudices and accept her as an equal partner.

She forked up the last of her steak, drained her glass, and ordered apple pie as she watched him from beneath lowered lashes.

Yes, very attractive. Perhaps one day they might get together. The day Lee accepted her as an equal.

Back in their room Fisher poured two glasses of imported brandy. It was part of the cover, and he enjoyed the feeling of luxury it gave him.

Also, the liquor slipped down easily, with a pleasant burning sensation.

He explained what had happened, outlining Farrow's talk of money-making gangs and the little man's promise to make contact.

"We'll have to let Brad know," said Emma. "He might get a lead in Northville."

"They have to contact me first," warned Lee.

"So I need to stay around, and I'm not letting you head off to Northville. Wouldn't look right anyway."

Emma agreed: it made sense.

"Best thing," he said, "is to stick around and wait to see what happens. If Farrow doesn't show up, I'll look some more. If I can get in with Farrow, I should be all right with the other groups. Either way, we need to know who's hitting at Wilde before we contact McGarry."

"All right," nodded Emma, "let's wait. We'll give it a week. If nothing happens by then we'll have to think of something else."

They finished the brandy and Emma made for the inner chamber. Lee moved to follow, but the door closed too fast, the click of the turning key sounding loud as his hand dropped to the knob.

"Sorry, *sweetheart*," called Emma, "but you sleep out there. I need some rest."

Fisher grinned, pouring a fresh measure of brandy.

One day, he thought. One day soon.

4

INDEPENDENCE looked good in the morning. Sunlight sparked bright off the water of the Missouri, outlining the tall shapes of buildings, the high pilot houses of the river boats, throwing long shadows down the main street.

The town came awake earlier than Fisher, and he sat up on the divan to the screaming of whistles off the river and the rattle of hooves and wheels from the street.

He pulled on his pants and padded barefoot over to the door. Slapping his palm against the wood, he called for Emma to wake up, standing back as a muffled voice answered, followed by a rustle of clothing and the sound of bare feet on carpet.

Turning away, he gathered up the blanket he had used, patting the cushions back into place.

"Morning," he said brightly as the door opened. "Sleep well?"

Emma nodded, holding a dark blue robe closed over her nightdress. Her auburn hair was

52

let down and she swept a cluster of wayward locks from her face, blinking at the light streaming in through the big windows.

"Coffee?" asked Fisher.

Emma nodded. "And hot water."

The Creole Palace ran to the unusual luxury of a bell system connecting the more expensive rooms with the servants quarters. Lee Fisher smiled as he tugged on the cord: he wasn't accustomed to such excellent service. Yet.

A while later there was a rap on the door and he pulled it open. A Negro stood outside with a big pot of hot water clutched in his arms.

"Mornin' suh." He was old, crinkly hair white, his back stooped over. "Brought you some nice hot water, suh."

"Thanks," said Fisher, stepping back.

The Negro walked slowly into the room, setting the big jug down on the central table with a nervous sigh. He looked too frail to carry so large a vessel, and Fisher studied his face, trying to figure out his age.

"You like some coffee, suh? Won't take but a moment to fetch it."

"Yeah, please," nodded Fisher.

"Right away, suh. You just wait a moment an' I'll be right back."

Fisher closed the door behind the Negro, wondering how a man could act so nervous when he was just doing a job. Then he thought about Jubal Farrow and the way the blacks stepped aside to make room for white men to pass. And decided it was probably a means of staying alive and unharmed.

And a rotten way to live.

He went back into the room to carry the jug through to Emma.

Too thoughtful to continue their usual banter, he simply set the pot down by the wash-basin and left her alone. She looked at him curiously, wondering why he was so silent, but thought better of asking him as he slumped on the divan.

After a while the coffee came, carried in by the same old Negro. He set the big wooden tray down on the table and studiously arranged the two cups and the silvered sugar bowl and cream jug in the centre.

"Breakfast's servin' now, suh," he said, shuffling back to the door. "Best be gettin' down if you want the pick."

Fisher muttered something, digging in his pocket for a coin. He didn't bother checking the size, just tossed it to the man.

It must have have been a half-dollar at least, because the old man smiled hugely, bobbing his head almost to his knees as he backed out of the room.

Fisher poured a cup of the strong black coffee, feeling an aftertaste of the disgust Jubal Farrow had raised in him. If this was what slavery was about, then he sided with the abolitionists. And he was going to enjoy this job even less than he had thought—luxury living or not.

He waited until Emma told him the wash-basin was clear and went in to wash up and shave, still lost in his private thoughts.

When he was finished and they were both dressed, he escorted Emma down to the dining-room for breakfast.

He was pleasantly aware that they made a handsome couple. Emma wore a rich brown outfit, the flare-waisted jacket emphasising her figure, the colour setting off her hair and complexion. Fisher himself was dressed in a suit he had had made in St. Louis, black and cut tight. His pants were tucked into boots gleaming bright from the ministrations of the night porter, the black leather matching the use-polished sheen of his gunbelt. The two pounds nine ounces of the .36 calibre Navy Colt sat comfortably on his right hip, wash leather pouches holding percussion caps and the lead balls. A powder flask hung alongside the pouches and in the pockets of his jacket, he carried twenty to thirty ready-made cartridges.

Dipping his head, he murmured a polite greeting to the room in general, then eased back Emma's chair before sitting down himself.

They were finishing the last of their eggs when Fisher noticed a man watching them. Habit had assured him of a table set back against one wall of the dining-room, where he could watch the entire room without exposing his back. It was habit, too, that sent his eyes wandering over the other tables as he ate. The kind of habit that keeps a man alive.

The watcher was young—about Fisher's age —and dressed in a cheap-looking broadcloth suit of a grey that didn't quite match the colour of the derby pushed back over curly, brown hair. Fisher checked him out with automatic precision: no sign of a gunbelt, nor much indication of a shoulder holster. Though that did not preclude a hide-away gun.

Fisher reached for his napkin, using the

movement to slip the hammer thong off his Colt.

He kept his right hand on his hip as the man walked towards them, pouring coffee with his left.

"Someone's coming to talk to us," he murmured to Emma. "If I start to move, get out of the way."

Emma nodded, and Fisher was obliged to applaud her calm. She resisted the temptation to turn around, simply smiling as she set her bag on the table and pretended to rummage through the contents.

Fisher knew that her hand was on the little derringer, and guessed that the hammer was drawn back ready to fire.

The curly-haired man smiled as he approached. Fisher eased his hand over the Colt's grip, letting his thumb rest on the hammer.

"Morning, folks." The newcomer lifted his derby. With his left hand, Fisher noticed. "Mr. Fisher, ma'am."

He appeared slightly nervous, as though unsure of his welcome. Or his chances.

"Morning," said Fisher politely. "Can I help you?"

The hammer of the Colt was back to half-cock.

"Sure hope so," grinned the stranger. "I'd better introduce myself. Matt Granger. I work for the Independence *Star-Bugle*. We generally run a piece on anyone new in town; it fills up the blank pages."

Fisher eased the hammer back down: a newspaperman.

"Take a seat," he said pleasantly. "Coffee?"

"Be real welcome." Granger pulled an empty chair over.

"Why us?" Fisher asked. "There must be hundreds of people coming into town with better stories to tell."

Granger smiled. "Oh, there's plenty of people passin' through, but I heard that you've booked a suite for an indefinite period. Anyway, you look a might different to the usual travellers."

Emma smiled graciously. Fisher said nothing. Granger waited a moment, then went on with professional enthusiasm.

"Fact is, we like to run a story on anyone settling here. You know the kind of thing: new business starting up, the town growing, attracting people. And with all this border

58

raiding it's gotten so that we don't get too many honest folks coming in."

"How long have the raids been going on?" asked Fisher, the innocent citizen.

Granger shrugged. "All summer. Least, there was some outlawry before that, but since the slavery question got to be a big issue things hotted up. After the riots in Lawrence and the killings down on Pottawatomie Creek, it all kind of ran away."

He sipped his coffee, then pulled a notebook from inside his jacket. Producing a thick, chewed pencil, he licked the tip and glanced at Fisher.

"Now if you fine people don't mind answering a few questions?"

"Go ahead," said Fisher. "Ask away."

The item appeared three days later. The *Star-Bugle* was a four-page broadsheet, smaller than the St. Louis papers, but the most important journal in Independence. It was as good a way as any to announce their presence in the town, and Fisher hoped that Jubal Farrow or his mysterious friends would spot the article.

"Mister L. Fisher has chosen the fair city of

59

Independence as his home for a while" [it read]. "Mr. Fisher arrived on Monday, having travelled up river from St. Louis, where he was recently living. Mr. Fisher is a Southern gentleman of private means, who previously spent some years exploring our North-western territories.

"Accompanying Mr. Fisher during his sojourn amongst us is his charming friend Miss Emma Wright. Miss Wright . . ."

It went on in the same vein for several paragraphs, part fact, part fantasy made up on the spot by Fisher, or later by the reporter.

Lee read it aloud to Emma, grinning.

"I never knew," he remarked, "there were so many ways to say *mistress*. I guess that's being polite."

"Or hospitable," replied Emma, smiling. "Let's hope it brings your friend out into the open."

Fisher hoped so too. They had been in town the better part of a week and while their relationship seemed to be improving, their chances of infiltrating the raiding parties weren't. There had been no sign of Farrow, nor any approach made by his mysterious friends.

Lee had stayed clear of the Glory Hole, and none of the other saloons had revealed the man. He was beginning to think it might be an idea to ride over to Northville and check with McGarry.

The break came the day the newspaper was published.

They were sitting in the lounge of the Creole Palace drinking coffee when a Negro brought a message.

Fisher took the envelope off the silver tray and peered at the waxed seal. Ripping it open, he pulled out a single sheet of paper. The hand was firm and flowing, curlicues spilling around the letters like decorations. It was an invitation to dine with a Mr. Charles Beaumont and friends. Fisher checked the date: it was that night. There was a postscript, saying that Mr. Beaumont would send a man to guide them, calling for them at six; if it was inconvenient, they should simply leave a message with the desk clerk.

He passed the note over to Emma, his dark eyes thoughtful.

"Might be something," he said. "Then again, it could be a purely social thing."

"There's only one way to find out," answered Emma.

"Yeah." Fisher nodded. "We'll be ready at six. Before then I think I'll see what I can discover about Mr. Beaumont."

He drained his cup and stood up.

"Why don't you go buy a dress, or something? I'll take a stroll down to the newspaper offices and see what I can dig up."

Emma nodded her agreement, too pleased with the possibility of getting a lead at last to argue with being left behind. Fisher strode out of the room, his hunter's instinct tingling warnings through the short hairs of his neck. It's probably nothing, he told himself, just some old gentleman who likes to keep in touch with events in St. Louis. It'll be a boring dinner that gets us nowhere.

Matt Granger changed his mind.

The reporter was settled into a swivel-back chair when Fisher pushed in through the decorated glass doors of the *Star-Bugle* offices, his feet up on the desk in front of him and his sleeves rolled up to protect them from the ink on his hands. He was reading over a page of rough copy.

He grinned at Fisher, holding up his palms to show why he didn't shake hands.

"Hi, there. What can I do for you? We got something wrong? Jim's not the best type-setter around."

A grey-haired man snorted from behind a big hand-set press and Fisher smiled.

"No. The piece was fine. Real fine. I came in to ask you some questions for a change."

"Ask away," grinned Granger. "It's all part of the service."

"I been invited to dinner," said Fisher. "Got a note just now from someone called Charles Beaumont. I'd like to know who he is, what he means around here."

Granger looked surprised. "You never heard of ole Charley Beaumont? I thought that you and him would be old friends, being Southerners and all."

Fisher shrugged. "No. I don't recall the man."

"Charles Fremantle Beaumont," said Granger solemnly, "is the biggest landowner around these parts. He's owner of a good third of Independence, with more land outside. He raises cows and corn, cattle and slaves. You name it, Beaumont has a finger in it. I never understood why he settled out here. The family comes from South Carolina, still owns land down there, I believe. Real Southern gentlefolk."

He said it bitterly, then looked embarrassed as he recalled Fisher's supposed origins. Hiding it, he turned away to a bureau set back against one wall of the office. Shoving long strips of proofed type aside, he pulled out a file.

"Charles Beaumont," he read. "Born in Tasker, South Carolina, 1805. That makes him 52. Came to Missouri around 1847 and started buying land. Built it all up into the biggest operation this side of Robert Wilde's holdings in Kansas."

Fisher's nerves tingled, but he kept a straight face.

"Slave owner. Firm believer in white supremacy. Family's friendly with James Buchanan, even put money into his election campaign. Beaumont is solid on the slavery ticket, made a few speeches about it. There's something else . . . Yes. There was talk of him harbouring a jayhawker one time. Man called James. Caleb James. Beaumont hired a lawyer —from Virginia—and James got off."

Granger closed the file and looked up.

"That's all we know about him."

"That's plenty," said Fisher. "Thanks a lot."

"Pleasure," answered the reporter. "I guess I shouldn't have given you the information, but I got a feeling you don't like slavery anymore than me."

Fisher just smiled and turned for the door.

"You be dining with Beaumont?" Granger called after him.

"I guess," said Fisher.

"Well," called the other man, "it won't be the first time I was wrong."

Fisher shut the door. There were times he didn't enjoy working undercover.

The Beaumont place was one of the biggest he had ever seen. Following the Negro outrider in through the wide, wrought-iron gates he took time to study the grounds. They spread out on both sides of the wide drive, the white-painted walls fading off into the distance behind stands of spruce and larch trees, the lawns trimmed down to a uniform neatness. There was a brook running musically through the grass to his right, its banks shelved tidily into the same conformity that dominated the landscape surrounding the house.

And that was a real surprise.

A flight of wide, white steps lead up to a verandah, roofed over with smooth, blue-shining tiles. Above the tiles, a balcony surrounded the first storey of the building. Above the balcony rose two more floors, terminating in a slanting pagoda-tipped roof that overhung the house like a protective shield.

Granger, thought Fisher, hadn't been exaggerating when he said Beaumont had money.

A Negro manservant with a white-dyed wig covering his head confirmed the impression. He was dressed in a turn-of-the-century rig of braided coat and hip-hugging white pants, his hands covered by spotless gloves that almost matched his teeth.

"Please come this way, suh, marm." He bowed as he said it. "The master is waiting for you."

Another slave came out to take the rig and Fisher took Emma's arm as they followed the first man through a hall bigger than the cabin he lived in for the first five years of his life. The slave led them through wide doors that were opened by two more liveried servants, and called their names.

Across the room beyond, a man turned to greet them. He was tall and fat, his scalp showing through the thinly spread strands of his greying hair. Moist lips spread in a smile that looked professionally sincere as he walked over to shake Fisher's hand, kiss Emma's.

"Charles Beaumont at your service. I'm delighted you are able to attend."

"Our pleasure," said Fisher, acting his part. "It's a pleasure to meet a fellow Southerner."

Beaumont's piggy eyes twinkled, roving over the cleavage of Emma's dress as he answered. "The pleasure is mine, sir. We Southern folk must stick together in these troubled times."

"Right," said Fisher. "There's enough people against us."

Beaumont muttered something in reply, steering them over towards the other guests as Fisher studied the room with professional interest. Wide doors opened on to lawns at the rear, the glass reflecting the light of the chandeliers hanging from the ceiling. Clustered about the doors were ten or more people, mostly men. They looked to be local dignitaries of one kind or another, middle-aged and running to fat. But two caught his attention.

One was a tall, bearded man, looking ill at ease in a badly-fitting jacket and dress shirt. The other was thin and pale, the sheen of his black hair matching the gloss of his boots. Fisher noted the bulge under the pale man's left arm; the spread of cloth over the other's hips, where side holsters bulked out his loose coat.

He shook hands, smiling pleasantly.

"Jonas Vickers," said Beaumont. "An old friend of mine. And my foreman, Caleb James."

Fisher went through the rituals of introduction, hoping that Emma would remember the names and faces. There were only two who interested him: Caleb James because Matt Granger had mentioned the man's name in connection with Beaumont, and Jonas Vickers.

Why the pale man fascinated him so much, he could not say. There was something about Vickers that stank of death. Talking to him was like hearing a rattlesnake clatter its tail in his mind, looking at him was like staring into the eyes of a death's head. Fisher kept a fixed smile plastered over his face and acted the part of Southern gentleman.

He kept it up throughout the meal, ignoring the stares of James and the less obvious glances of Vickers and Beaumont. It wasn't too difficult: Emma was seated on his right and a pretty blonde girl to his left. The blonde was clearly interested, and he enjoyed her flirtatious chatter —enjoyed even more the way Emma resented it.

It was almost disappointing when the servants brought in the decanters of port and two boxes of cigars, and Beaumont suggested that the ladies withdraw.

Fisher accepted a glass of the dark, rich wine, and settled back in his chair, waiting for someone to open the conversation.

It came from Vickers, to his surprise.

"I heard you had a spot of trouble at the Glory Hole."

Fisher laughed: "Hardly trouble. I stopped by for a drink and happened in on an argument. I just helped out the side I thought was in the right."

Vickers and Beaumont exchanged glances.

"You thought it was worth risking your life to help them?" asked Beaumont. "That was taking a chance, no?"

Fisher shrugged. "If you believe in something, you should stand up for it."

"But you might have been killed," urged the fat man.

"I might have been killed a whole lot of times," said Fisher. "I'm still alive, though."

"Way I heard it," said Vickers softly, "was that you grabbed a shotgun and backed the whole damn' saloon off. That was some long chance."

"Would you risk a scattergun in your face?" asked Fisher. "I wouldn't."

Caleb James erupted into sudden laughter. "What the hell did I tell you? I said he was one fer us. Jubal told me all about it. This man's got grit to spare."

"Yes," murmured Beaumont. "It would appear so."

He filled his third glass, handing the decanter on to the man at his left, raising the brimming goblet in Fisher's direction.

"I give you a toast, gentlemen. To a new recruit."

70

5

EMMA paced the room in a fury of impatience. Fisher grinned as he towelled his face dry and tossed the cloth on to the wash-stand. He poured a glass of brandy and tugged his tie loose, opening his collar before turning to face her.

"Well? What happened?" She tapped an irritable heel as she said it. "You were closeted with them long enough, now let me in on your secrets."

"I'm one of them," said Lee. "That stuff in the paper convinced them; almost. Farrow had told them I was on their side, so they wanted to check me out. Beaumont made enough hints to convince me they'll set something up to prove it."

"Almost?" said Emma.

"Sure. They think I'm one more sympathiser looking to make some fast money in a good cause. They won't be sure until I prove myself, but that shouldn't be difficult. I'm waiting to hear what they got in mind. Vickers promised

71

to contact me with a proposition. When he does, I just go along with it and find out who's hitting Wilde."

"It sounds easy," said Emma.

"It is," grinned Fisher.

"Too easy," added the woman. "I think they'll set you up for something."

Fisher shrugged, tugging the strap of his holster loose from his thigh. He unbuckled the gunbelt and dropped it on the divan.

"Like what?" he asked. "I can act the outlaw if that's what they want."

"Lee," said Emma. Urgently. "You don't understand it, do you? If they think you're one of them, they'll want you to go with them on a raid. That could mean burning out a farmer. Maybe driving him off his land."

Fisher emptied his glass and set it down on the table. His face became suddenly serious. "Listen," he said. "We came out here to do a job. It's not pleasant, and I'd sooner call Beaumont and the others out. Kill them on the street and be done with it. But we don't operate that way. I can't be sure they're the ones getting at Wilde. Not yet. I think they are, but that's to be found out. If I can be sure, I got no reason not to kill them. If I ride with them, maybe I can save that farmer's life. At the very least, I can line them up for trial."

"Oh, dammit," said Emma. "Sometimes I hate this job."

She turned towards him, and he thought for a moment that there were tears in her eyes. He reached towards her, resting his hands gently on her shoulders.

"We're in it now, like it or not," he said.

"Right now I don't." She leaned her head forwards against his arm. "Take care, Lee. Promise me."

Fisher was beginning to think that he was getting somewhere when Emma pulled away. Embarrassed by her unusual show of affection, she stared at his face, then turned and went into the bedroom. Fisher smiled and moved to follow her, but the sound of the key turning halted him and he stopped.

Maybe it's better this way, he thought. If Emma got emotional, she could make his job that much harder. Afterwards. When it was done with and they were back in St. Louis. It would wait until then . . .

He stripped off his shirt and eased his boots from his feet. It was as good a reason as any for finishing this assignment fast.

He slept well that night, and in the morning there was word from Beaumont.

The fat man wanted to see him, would buy him a drink that evening in a saloon called the Lost Dog.

Fisher pushed through the batwing doors soon after sundown, pausing inside to survey the room. The saloon was crowded, most of the space taken up by card tables and the big chance wheel that was spinning brightly at the far end. The room was thick with smoke and the clinking of glasses, hanging kerosene lanterns spilling yellow light through the haze. A balcony ran around three walls, and halfway down the room there was a staircase leading up to the rooms above.

Caleb James was sipping whisky at the bar. Fisher moved to join him.

"I been waitin' for you." The bearded man emptied his glass. "Let's go."

He lead the way over to the stairs, motioning for Lee to follow him. Up on the balcony he halted outside a door and knocked twice. A familiar voice called for them to enter and Lee stepped into the unexpected luxury of Jason Vickers' room.

The thin man was standing beside a low

74

table, his back to the door. Charles Beaumont was leaning back against a settle, glass in one hand and a cigar in the other. They looked like they had been arguing.

"Welcome." Vickers managed to make the greeting sound like an invitation to a hanging. "What'll you drink?"

"Whisky," said Fisher.

Vickers poured two generous shots and passed them across. Caleb James took his and moved over to the window. Beaumont smiled, and Fisher waited. Vickers broke the silence.

"You changed your mind about throwing in with us?"

Lee shook his head. "No."

"All right, we'll give you a chance to show you mean it. We're riding tonight . . ."

"Hold on," interrupted Fisher. "There was a whole lot of loose talk last night about supporting the South and hitting at the yankees. We never did get around to one other important question: what's in it for me?"

Beaumont spluttered something about loyalty and duty, but Vickers waved him to silence, a tight smile spreading across his narrow lips.

"You're good, Fisher. You know that?" He

refilled their glasses. "I like a man who speaks his mind; it lets me know where he stands."

Fisher shrugged. "I got to make a living like anyone else."

"That's fair enough," rustled Vickers, "and you will with us."

"Not by raiding dirt farmers," said Lee. "Where's the profit in that?"

Vickers smiled some more. "You underestimate us, my friend. The farmers we attack are just part of a larger organisation. Hitting them, we hit the man at the top."

"Who is?" Fisher queried.

"In time," said Vickers, "you'll find out. For now, you're on probation. Prove yourself and you'll be told as much as anyone."

"Yeah," grunted Lee. "That makes sense, but you still haven't said where the money comes in."

"Do you know how much a slave is worth?" asked Vickers.

"Of course," replied Fisher, hoping he wouldn't be asked to name the price.

He wasn't: the cadaverous outlaw was launched on a lecture.

"We run off a great many Negroes. The owners—if they're still alive—assume the blacks have fled, or been killed. We herd them across the river and sell them. It brings in a great deal of money.

"We also use the opportunities presented by these difficult times to rob—sorry, Charles—to *liberate* those banks or stage coaches showing sympathy to the North. Part of the money is sent to Richmond, the remainder is divided amongst us."

"Now that," said Fisher approvingly, "makes sense."

"I thought it might," murmured Vickers. "Charles here does not quite approve, but then he has money of his own. An army pays its soldiers, and if you join us, Fisher, you will be a soldier in the army of the South."

Fisher grinned, lifting his glass in a mock salute.

"I'm enrolled," he said.

The gang met a mile out of town at a disused lumber mill. Fisher counted upwards of twenty men, Jubal Farrow among them, all heavily armed. Vickers, dressed in a heavy black riding-coat, shouted for silence. It came instantly.

"We got a new recruit, men." His dry voice

carried in the, silence. "Name's Lee Fisher. Let's show him how we operate."

A few men greeted Lee with handshakes and murmured words of encouragement, but most of them just sat their horses, waiting for Vickers and Caleb James to lead out. When the skeletal man turned his horse west and heeled it up to an easy canter, the others fell into line behind him, riding two abreast like a military column. Fisher noticed that many of them wore the maroon shirts he had seen around Independence.

He urged his own mount forwards, riding up to come alongside of Vickers.

"Where we headed?" he asked.

Vickers stared ahead as he replied. "There's a fair-sized spread 'tween here and Lawrence. Run by a man called Knowles. The Butterfield stage uses his place as a way station, and it's due in tonight. With a strongbox on board."

"What's in the box?" asked Fisher.

"Around ten thousand dollars," said Vickers calmly.

Fisher whistled, long and low. "Soldier's pay."

"Yeah," chuckled Vickers. "Something like that."

Fisher pulled back, falling into line with his mind working furiously. It was pretty clear that the raid would have a violent climax: no-one was going to hand over ten thousand dollars without a fight. His problem was to decide how to handle himself. If he pulled out of the fighting, Vickers would want to know why. If he acted out his part, he might be required to kill innocent men.

It was a problem without a handy solution.

Lee Fisher had no compunction about killing. That, so far as he was concerned, was a natural part of life. Times were when a gun was the only answer, and the man in the right was the man who drew first. It was Lee's practice to be the first.

Shooting up a ranch to rob a stage-coach was something else. Something that ran against the grain of his conscience. He wondered if there was a way around the problem.

He couldn't think of one.

They reached the Knowles holding a little before midnight. Lights showed from the windows of a squat, timber building, throwing shadows off the bulk of the coach parked alongside the door. Vickers halted his men a quarter-mile out from the stockyards and began to issue orders.

Five men eased forwards, walking their horses quietly towards the ranch. Their job was to run off the stock penned in the yards. Five others were sent to cover the rear and side of the place. Two men were told off to handle the gang's horses and the remainder drifted down the gentle slope fronting the building.

"You stick with me," murmured Vickers. "When we go in, just start firing. Knowles'll have about seven men in there with him. The stage usually carries a few passengers, so there could be up to six more. Them and the driver and guard. Kill them before they get a chance to reach a gun."

"Sure," said Fisher.

They rode slowly down the slope, dismounting before the penned horses got scent of their own animals and moving in on foot.

Vickers led the way, Caleb James on his right, hefting the sawed-off Meteor, Lee on his left.

They reached the front of the building and men peeled off to cover the windows. Vickers drew a Navy Colt from beneath his jacket and cocked the .36 calibre pistol. He turned to

Caleb and jerked his head at the door. The bearded man grinned, stepping forwards.

He kicked the oak boards hard, then stepped back, cocking the shotgun.

Fisher took a deep breath, abruptly aware of the dryness in his mouth. Dammit, he thought, I'm in this now, like it or not. There's only one way to go, and that's forwards.

The door opened, the light from inside illuminating a tall man wearing faded trousers held up by wide braces. He carried a Colt's Dragoon in his right hand. The gun, Fisher noticed, was not cocked.

Then Caleb's shotgun went off.

The man flew backwards, lifted off his feet by the close-range blast. He screamed once as his stomach tore apart, splashing blood over Caleb's shirtfront and face. The big man ignored it, jumping through the door with Vickers and Lee close behind him.

The shotgun roared again, and two men pitched over, their faces bloody.

Vickers was laughing as he fired into the men huddled around the central table. There were nine of them and they were taken completely by surprise. Three went down as Vickers' men opened fire from the windows, bullets hitting

81

them from three sides so that they twisted about as they died, like puppets when the strings are tugged at random. Two more made a run for the rear door. Vickers fired twice. The men seemed to spurt forwards, crashing against the door and bouncing off. Where they had touched the woodwork, there were great smears of crimson.

Lee levelled his gun. Squeezed the trigger. And hoped that Vickers hadn't seen the bullet blast splinters from the table. He fired again, chipping stone from the chimney.

The defenders had the table tipped over now and Fisher risked planting bullets in the heavy wood. One. Two. Three . . .

Then the metallic *click* of the hammer striking an empty cylinder.

Grateful, he ducked back around the door to reload.

Vickers was already there, pinching percussion caps over the nipples of his Colt.

"Well?" he called to Lee. "You enjoying it?"

Fisher forced a grin. "Be better when we've got the money. That table's like a barricade."

"Yeah." Vickers triggered a shot round the doorway. "We'd best do something about that."

He shouted for Caleb and the big man

appeared out of the flaming night, his beard bloodied, his eyes grim. Vickers said something to him that Lee couldn't hear over the roar of the guns, and Caleb disappeared again.

When he reappeared, he was carrying a storm lantern.

Lee watched as Vickers struck a match and set it to the wick. There was a glow of pale blue flame, shading into yellow as the thin man adjusted the control screw. The lantern had a copper fuel drum and a wired-glass chimney sooted up from long usage. Vickers held the drum in his left hand, motioning for Caleb and Lee to shift to the left side of the door.

Then he hurled the lantern into the room.

The glass chimney shattered against the upper edge of the table. Kerosene splashed over the wood. Was lit by the wick. There was a *whoosh* of flame, and the whole surface of the table erupted in a great fireball of yellow and red.

A man screamed and stood up. Kerosene had splashed over his shirt and he was beating at the flames with his bare hands. Caleb triggered the shotgun. The man seemed to jump back, crashing into the fireplace with flames licking around the edges of the hole in his chest. His blood sizzled as it splashed over the flames.

Another man yelled something too slurred with fear to be understandable and tossed his gun over the burning table. Vickers shot him as he stood up, a neat head shot that tipped him back over the corpse in the fireplace.

Caleb's scattergun thundered again, blasting a chunk of splintered wood loose from the table. Vickers ducked around the doorway, fanning his gun. Then both outlaws drew back to reload.

Lee cursed as another man stood up. He held a Colt's Dragoon in his right hand and a Remington's Army model in his left. He was tall and hurting. Blood ran thick down his jaw, welling from a wide cut on his cheek. His hair was burning where the kerosene had splashed over his head, and one eye was closed and blistered. He fired the two handguns with practised skill, shouting curses as he moved out from behind the table. A rifle bullet jerked him sideways, spilling blood over his left hip, and then the window guns fell silent.

Lee stared at the macabre, burning figure, horribly aware of his predicament.

The man staggered across the room, still firing.

Fisher counted the shots: One. Two. Three. Four.

The Colt was empty, its hammer falling on a used cap.

One.

Two.

The Remington was still full-loaded, and the burning man was walking towards the door.

Fisher clamped his teeth tight and shoved the Colt out at arm's length.

There was no other sound than the crackle of the building fire and the thudding of the man's boots on the planks of the ranch-house. Vickers' men were either reloading like their leader, or waiting to see what the new recruit would do.

A bullet threatened to spoil Fisher's stetson. And the man was almost to the door.

Lee squeezed the trigger. Felt the Navy Colt buck in his hand.

The man grunted as the .36 calibre ball ploughed through his rib-cage. He doubled over, spitting blood, and went down on his knees. Reflex action had already cocked Fisher's pistol for a second shot and he held the Colt rock-steady on the man's chest.

Don't get up, thought Fisher. Please don't get up. You've got a couple of ribs busted, but that's all. You can crawl out of here and start up again. Your hair'll grow back and you'll be alive. Just don't get up!

The man pushed up to a kneeling position. He saw Fisher and began to lift the Remington. With a slowness that was as painful to Fisher as it was to his victim.

Aim . . .

Cock the hammer . . .

Squeeze the trigger . . .

Fisher fired first. His bullet exploded the sternum, blasting through thin bone into the lung beneath. The man pitched back, his pistol exploding a useless hole in the roof. He remained in the kneeling position with his spine canted back so that his head touched the boards behind him. Blood spilled from his mouth and chest and nostrils.

And Lee Fisher felt sick.

The flames had spread now, licking hungrily over the floor to lap at the walls. The overturned table was almost totally consumed, so that the one remaining man lost his cover. He realised the hopelessness of his position and hurled his gun away.

"All right! You got me!" His voice was tinged with hysteria. "I give up! I'm coming out."

"Knowles," grunted Vickers. "That's Frank Knowles."

The thin man stood up, peering round the door.

"All right, Knowles! Come on out."

The rancher nodded, lifting both hands up above his head.

"Don't shoot! I'm comin' out. You take the ranch, whatever you want. Just don't shoot."

"Sure," said Vickers.

And fired.

Knowles spun back with blood coming out of his chest. He began to double over, but Vickers' second bullet hit his face, smashing him upright again as he dribbled crimson froth over his stained shirt. He tottered for a moment before a third bullet shattered his collar-bone and he fell down.

"Get that damn' box," shouted Vickers. "Before it gets burned up."

Caleb and Lee ran into the house. The fire was not yet strong enough to repel them, but there was little time in which to find the strongbox. They looked around the room.

"There," grunted Caleb. "By the fire."

Lee followed the big man's gaze. The Butterfield box was next to the fireplace. A leg straddled the metal frame, blood dripping slowly from a hole in the knee. One side of the thing was almost red-hot where spilled kerosene and the tumbled remnants of Knowles' fire had splashed over the metal.

Fisher was faster than Caleb. He grabbed the cool end of the box, waiting as the big man fumbled for a glove.

Caleb was tugging the glove on to his left hand when the rear door opened and a woman stepped through.

She was short and dumpy, on the wrong side of middle-age, and looking angry. Her hair was grey, tumbled from sleep, and streaked with soot. She held a worn gown closed tight over her pendulous breasts and began to shriek as she saw the bodies spread around the room.

Caleb lifted the scattergun in his left hand. Fisher noticed that he used it as casually as a pistol. The right-hand hammer was thumbed back as the arm extended towards the woman. And the gun went off.

A full load of ought-ought shot reduced the woman's head to a mangled, bloody pulp. The force of the blast hurled her back the way she had come. Her body landed heavily on the boards of the room she had occupied, and from the lintel of the door there came a dipping of brain matter and shards of torn bone.

Caleb ignored her as he lifted the box. Fisher fought nausea as he followed on. And between them they wrestled the metal container outside.

Vickers was pleased with the results.

He sent men to call the other outlaws in and set to breaking open the strongbox. One of Knowles' horses was used to carry the gold, tipped into two big panniers spread over a pack-horse held in check by Caleb James.

As they rode away from the burning ranch Lee asked when the money would be split up.

Vickers laughed. "Tomorrow," he said, "along with the horses. I'll tell you what your part is."

Fisher nodded. He didn't feel like saying anything; only like killing Vickers and Caleb and the others on the spot.

"You handled that real well," said the thin man. "I do believe you're one of us, pure an' genuine."

"Sure as hell he is," added James. "You see him hit that dumb bastard with the two guns?

He let him suffer then fed him a twosome o' lead that put him where he belongs."

Lee grinned, trying hard to look pleased with himself.

It was difficult to smile with his teeth shut tight over the sickness in his gut, but he did his best. And it seemed that his companions accepted it.

He hoped so; because otherwise he was a dead man.

6

BRADFORD McGARRY got Lee Fisher's message three days later.

He was glad to receive it because he was getting bored in Northville. Since meeting Robert Wilde he had done nothing more than hang around the rancher with one hand close to his gun. And that got tedious after a while.

Wilde had explained the systematic raiding of his farms; shown McGarry columns of figures that itemised the financial losses involved when cabins were burned down and Negroes—in Wilde's case, free labourers paid a moderate wage for a day's work—were killed or scared off. The columns read like a planned programme of extermination: someone was aiming to take over the Wilde holdings.

Who was another matter.

Fisher's note didn't explain the situation clearly, but it did give McGarry an idea of who might be behind the raids. So the third member of the Agency began to form his own plans.

And the first step was to talk with Fisher.

Somewhere lonesome and secret, where they could put into words what couldn't go into a stage-coach's mailbags.

McGarry decided to take a trip over to Independence.

He reached the town four days later, seven after the raid on the Knowles spread. Feelings were running high in Kansas by then. Thirteen people had been killed in the attack, one of them a woman. The anti-slavery citizens of Northville and Lawrence were talking about getting up their own vigilante groups to fend off the pro-slavery raiders, and homesteaders were arming up against fresh attacks without political discussion.

McGarry hoped he could reach his fellow agents before the whole damn' thing blew itself wide open.

"What in the damn' hell are you doing here?"

Fisher sounded as angry as he felt.

"I needed to talk with you."

"You know it could blow the whole thing apart? I thought you were the big undercover man. The one who never showed a sign. If Vickers or James spots you here I'm just so much target material. Emma too. They'll not stop at killing her."

"Will you calm down and listen?" McGarry was feeling irritable. "I spent two nights on the trail to see you. And it was your note brought me here."

"Christ!" grunted Fisher. "All the note said was did you know Frank Knowles, and was he anything to do with Wilde? You could've sent the answer back on the stage."

"Yeah, sure," said McGarry. "I could've done that. Only how would it leave me for an answer?"

"Waiting," said Fisher. "Same as me."

He was pleased that Emma was out taking tea with the ladies of the town. Partly because he didn't want her involved in the possibilities of someone spotting McGarry leaving his room, but mostly because he thought she might side with Brad.

"Listen," he said, "Jason Vickers has accepted me as one of the gang. He leads it along with a man called Caleb James. There's a Southerner—Charles Fremantle Beaumont— who looks like he's putting up the money to keep it all going. He's a true-blue Southerner;

as honest as that lets him be. Vickers and James look like the real leaders."

He grinned, weighing McGarry's conscience against his own.

"I could kill them. It wouldn't be difficult. But there wouldn't be any more proof than my word. And Beaumont wasn't even on the raid."

McGarry waved his right hand in a negative gesture.

"That's no good. If we wanted straight killings, Wilde could've set it up. He's got the money and the hate; could've handled it all himself. He wants more than that. He sides with the North, wants to see an end put on black slavery. For that to go through properly we have to produce firm evidence. Enough to convict your Jayhawkers."

"So leave me to it," said Fisher. "I'm in now. One of them. Let me find out what they're planning, and then I'll tell you. Maybe we can set up an ambush. It depends on the timing."

"All right," said McGarry. Reluctantly. "But keep me informed. I want to know what's going on."

"Sure," said Fisher. "I'll do that."

McGarry felt embarrassed, and that made him angry with himself. He had broken his rules in coming to see Fisher and even though he was sure no-one had seen him coming in, there was no way of knowing that he wouldn't be spotted leaving. In itself, talking with Fisher could be quite innocent; the danger lay in the possibility that someone might recognise him as Wilde's bodyguard. And that would leave Fisher wide open.

The brown-haired man covered his annoyance with a question.

"When's the next raid?"

Fisher shrugged. "I don't know. It seems like Vickers sends word just before. He keeps pretty close-mouthed about things until the gang's on its way."

"How about the proceeds?" asked McGarry. "Do you meet up for the split?"

"No." Fisher shook his head. "Leastways, not so far as I know. It seems like Vickers and James handle the financial end, then James delivers the money to everyone. He gave me two hundred dollars: my share of the Knowles raid."

"What you do with it?" McGarry queried. "That's stolen money."

"I'm spending it," answered Fisher, smiling at his companion's righteousness. "What else?"

"But it's stolen," protested McGarry. "It's not your money to spend."

"What am I supposed to do?" grunted Fisher. "I'm meant to be one of them, remember? It'd look kind of odd if I didn't use my share."

"I still don't like it," protested McGarry. "It's not right."

"Think of what I'm saving the Agency," grinned Fisher. "This way the Chief won't need to pay expenses."

McGarry started to say something more, but changed his mind. He knew from past experience that Fisher would go his own way, no matter what arguments were thrown against him. Instead, he asked about the actual selling operation.

"I don't have that worked out yet," said Lee. "Vickers keeps a tight mouth, and he's not the kind of man to be pushed into a thing. My guess is that Beaumont's place is used as a front. He owns slaves, so if Vickers' gang runs blacks across the river, they can be hidden on Beaumont's land and sold off later." He shrugged. "The same probably happens with the horses."

"So we could nail Beaumont for receiving

stolen property," murmured McGarry, thoughtful. "If we can get proof."

"I can take a look around," suggested Fisher, "but what happens if I do find some changed brands? A Missouri court won't convict Charles Fremantle Beaumont, and I'd have to give evidence. That'd leave Vickers and the rest in the clear."

"Yeah," said McGarry. "We need something more."

Abruptly, he changed tack.

"Who's the real leader? Beaumont or Vickers?"

"Hard to say," answered Fisher. "Beaumont looks like the genuine Southern gentleman and he knows all about the raids, but he seems to take orders from Vickers. Caleb James is just muscle. My feeling is that Vickers heads things. Beaumont goes along with it because it helps the South, and Vickers lets it look like Beaumont heads the thing."

"I'll see what I can find out about Vickers," said McGarry. "If the Chief's got anything on him worth knowing, I'll get in touch with you."

"Yeah, sure," nodded Fisher. "But meanwhile what happens? How do we break them up?"

McGarry paused, letting the idea that had been forming in his mind since Fisher's message arrived take clear shape.

"We need to catch them in the act," he murmured. "If I knew where and when they planned to hit next I could maybe arrange for the Army to be waiting."

"It's a nice idea," said Lee, "but how the hell do we work it? If Vickers only tells us where we're going as we ride out how can I get word to you?"

It was McGarry's turn to shrug. "That's up to you, Lee. I guess we'll have to play it by ear. Right now, that's about all we can do."

"Yeah," said Fisher, "I guess so."

He didn't tell McGarry about killing the man at the Knowles place, and was grateful that the brown-haired man didn't ask him for details. Whether that was delicacy on McGarry's part or just a lack of interest, he didn't know. Or care. The killing had left a bitter aftertaste in his mouth, and he knew that it would take blood to wash it away. Vickers' blood. And James', too.

They arranged to meet in a week's time, in Lawrence, and McGarry slipped out the door, leaving Fisher to think about his own plans.

So far he had concentrated on acting the role of gentleman traveller, which was another way of saying that he idled his time away. Accompanied by Emma, he had shown his face in the three decent eating houses in town, played cards most nights and spent the days driving around in the buggy or attending seemingly-interminable social afternoons. The off-key tinklings of the would-be pianists of Independence were beginning to grate on his nerves, as was the need to remain constantly polite with people he despised. Beaumont had invited them twice more to dinner, but on each occasion it had been nothing more than a formal, social event.

In a twisted kind of way, Lee hoped that another raid was in the offing. At least it would relieve the boredom.

He was thinking about it when Emma got back.

"We're invited to dinner," she announced. "Seven o'clock at Beaumont's place."

Fisher grimaced. "Hell! Haven't we been polite to enough people already?"

"It's work," said Emma calmly. "And at least we get a decent meal out of it."

"Sure," grunted Lee, a thought suddenly taking shape, "and maybe more besides."

The dinner was a more personal affair than the previous functions. Beaumont presided, flanked by Lee and Emma. There were two other couples there, a banker and his wife, and a local horse trader accompanied by a blowsy woman with a tarnished wedding band on her third finger. Conversation was limited to the price of cotton and of horses, with an occasional word about the political situation.

Fisher sensed that both the banker and the horse dealer had some idea of Beaumont's clandestine activities, but preferred to keep quiet and accept his money. That they sided with the South was obvious: Lee doubted they would be there were it otherwise. But their support, he guessed, was limited to talk and the odd contribution to campaign funds.

Beaumont got rid of them as soon as was decently possible, whispering to Fisher that he and Emma should stay around.

"Jonas wants to see you," he murmured as he poured brandy. "He needs your help again."

"He knows where to find me." Fisher stared

at the fat man over the rim of his goblet. "All he needs do is ask."

Beaumont glanced significantly at Emma, raising his eyebrows in silent question.

Fisher laughed. "Don't worry. Emma's on our side. She wouldn't be here otherwise."

Discreetly, Emma drifted away to the far end of the room and studied a painting.

"It's something big," whispered Beaumont. "Something that needs a real stranger to bring it off."

"What is it?" Fisher asked.

Beaumont grinned, licking his fat lips. "Jonas will tell you. He handles the military side of things. You go see him in his room, around noon tomorrow."

"Sure," agreed Fisher, wondering what was going on.

Emma rejoined the two men and they drifted into small talk as Beaumont's cigar burned smaller and the decanter of brandy slowly emptied.

"There's a great day coming." Beaumont slurred his words as the alcohol took affect. "It won't be long now, and I'm real glad to know that folks like you two are on our side."

"What day's that?" asked Emma. Innocently.

"Why, honey." Beaumont waved the stub of his cigar in the air. "The day the South rises, of course. We're laying the ground out here. Getting ready for the jubilee, you might say."

Fisher poured more brandy into the fat man's glass: this was getting interesting.

"It can't go on much longer," announced Beaumont. "The goddam government—beg your pardon, ma'am—ain't in no position to tell the South what to do. This slavery question is so much yankee bullshit. The North's worried about losing its influence, knows that we got the crops and the cotton. And the labour to handle it all. Dammit to hell! If the South decided to quit the Union tomorrow, we'd do real well for ourselves. England would support us—they need our Southern cotton—and there'd be more besides."

"You think it'll happen?" asked Fisher, genuinely curious.

"Sure do!" exclaimed Beaumont. "Why else are folks like us, you and me, fighting now? I'll tell you why. We're fighting for something we believe in. For the right to make up our own minds. And there's no goddam yankee can do that for us."

"Amen," said Fisher, hoping the sarcasm didn't show in his voice.

Soon after, he made excuses to leave. Beaumont wanted them to stay, to help him finish the second bottle of brandy, but Lee pleaded his meeting with Vickers and the need for a clear head. Reluctantly, the fat man let them go.

Outside the gates Lee hauled the buggy to a stop.

"Can you get back alone?" he asked.

"Of course," said Emma. "Where are you going?"

Lee grinned, swinging to the ground.

"I want to take a look around, see if our friend's hiding anything."

Before Emma could reply he was gone into the shadows.

7

FISHER scaled the wall easily. It was more for decoration than protection, and he doubted it went all the way around Beaumont's land anyway. He had not seen guards on his earlier—official—visits, but he paused in the shadow of a rowan tree and listened until he was confident that he had not been spotted.

Then he moved towards the house.

Skirting around the main buildings, he moved silently to the stock pens. Beaumont had shown him over the spread, proud of the extent of his holdings and anxious to impress his new-found friend. To facilitate such boastings, the Southerner had located his stables close to the main house so that visitors might be easily provided with horses.

Fisher drifted around the pens, approaching the main stable from the side. A Negro was dozing against the wall, a Springfield carbine resting across his knees. There was a lantern beside his drooped head and from the way the moths fluttered about the pale flame, Fisher could tell the man was sound asleep. He cat-footed forward, bunching his right hand to a fist.

He reached the guard and swung his fist, up and across. The shock ran through his arm and the Negro's head jerked sideways. Fisher grabbed the carbine before it clattered to the ground. He tugged the Negro upright again and replaced the gun. There was no sound from the stable, so he moved back to the corral.

Horses shifted nervously in the darkness. Fisher walked slowly towards them, whispering reassurances until he was in amongst them. He checked the brands. The first few carried Beaumont's Circle B. Then three showed with Frank Knowles' FK. Then Fisher found a pinto with a strange mark on its flank. He studied it in the pale moonlight. The brand had been doctored. Where Knowles' linked FK had been, a simple straight iron had been used to burn a bottom bar joining the base of the F to the bottom of the K. Then the outer angles of the K had been joined by the same bar to make a Box Arrow. It was an obvious change to someone who knew that Beaumont was taking in stolen animals, but with forged sale bills and a few witnesses—like

Caleb James—to back up the claim, Beaumont could easily sell the horses as bought-in stock.

Fisher checked over a few more animals before quitting the corral. He thought about checking over the slaves' quarters, but decided they were too far away. And people, unlike animals, were likely to be closer guarded. He reminded himself that horse stealing was still a hanging offence and began to think about getting back to the hotel.

Taking a horse was the obvious way to travel, but that would alert Beaumont. Fisher doubted that the Negro, when he came to, would risk punishment by telling his employer that he had been caught asleep. Especially not if there was nothing missing. He shrugged and set to walking.

Fisher got back to the hotel with sore feet and a worse temper. His boots weren't made for walking and by the time he limped in to Independence they felt like they were crushing his toes and doing their best to rub through to the bone of his heels. He took them off with a thankful sigh halfway down mainstreet.

His fob watch showed four in the morning, and the town was quiet. There was light shining from inside the Creole Palace, but all it lit up was Fisher and a thin-haired desk clerk sound asleep over the register.

He eased gently up the stairs and left his boots outside the door.

Emma was asleep, stayed that way as he slipped inside. He swallowed a glass of brandy, stripped off, and settled on the divan.

Emma woke him late the next morning.

"Coffee?"

Fisher nodded, sitting up. He remembered that he was naked and drew the sheet around his waist, rubbing at his eyes as the woman brought a steaming cup over to him.

"Thanks. I need that." He glanced at his watch: it was close on eleven. "I best get ready, after. If Vickers wants to see me at noon."

"Take a bath first," smiled Emma. "I took a look at your feet. They need bathing. What happened? You have to walk back?"

Fisher nodded. "Yeah. I should've asked you to wait around."

"Why didn't you?"

"Too dangerous," grunted Fisher, sipping the coffee. "Someone might have seen you. Anyway, hotels begin to wonder about ladies who stay out late. It was safer to do it alone."

Emma snorted. "One day, Lee, you'll accept that I know as much about this business as you. I've been doing it longer, remember. Still, what happened?"

"I saw a man about some horses," said Fisher, feeling better after the coffee. "Beaumont's got the herd we ran off the Knowles' place in his own yards. The brands are changed from FK to a Box Arrow. That should be enough to convict him."

"But not the others," said Emma.

"No," Fisher agreed. "We need to catch them red-handed."

He explained McGarry's plan along with the difficulties.

"Maybe Vickers will tell me something today," he said. "So that we can get word to McGarry."

Emma shook her head. "I doubt it. If he only tells you as you leave there's no way to alert Brad in time." She paused, thinking for a moment. "But there is another way. Suppose that I go to see Beaumont on my own? The way he tries to look down my dresses might just loosen his tongue. Suppose I got him to tell me their plans? He might talk to a woman he was planning to seduce. He's the kind of man who likes to look big."

"No," said Fisher. Irritably. "I don't like it. It's too dangerous."

Emma smiled, glancing down at Lee's watch.

"You'd best take that bath. You're due to see Vickers at noon."

Fisher went through to the tub. The water was still hot, and he wondered what excuses Emma had given the carriers as to why he was sleeping on the divan instead of the bed. He guessed that she had made some reasonable argument and then forgot about it as he sank into the hot water.

Forty minutes later he was dressed and shaved. His feet felt a whole lot better and the crisp strokes of the razor, allied with a clean shirt, had restored his confidence. He went out to see Vickers with a smile on his face.

The thin man's news dissolved his good humour.

"There's something big coming up," said Vickers, "and you're important to the whole plan. The lynch pin, you could say."

"What is it?" asked Fisher.

"You'll know later," was the only answer. "After you prove yourself."

"Prove myself?" said Fisher irritably. "What the hell do you mean? I proved myself at Knowles' place, didn't I? What more proof do you need?"

Vickers smiled, his deep-sunk eyes boring into Lee's face.

It was hard to decide whether he was being honest, or playing a game.

"We usually test strangers a couple of times. And besides, there's some of the boys say you held back on shooting. They want to see you handle something on your lonesome. Do that and you're in on the big one."

"Suppose I say no?" asked Fisher. "What then?"

Vickers had his jacket off, the straps of his shoulder holster showing dark against his ruffled shirt. The butt of the Colt's Navy model canted forwards from beneath his armpit.

His hand flashed sideways and the gun was aimed at Fisher's face.

"You die," he said.

Fisher stared hard at the muzzle of the pistol. It was rock-steady on his face; he avoided squinting down the barrel.

"What is this *test?*" He let his irritation show in his voice.

110

"You'll find out," said Vickers. "Just be ready at the old mill. At midnight."

Fisher was the first man there. Nobody else spoke much to him, most sitting their horses in uneasy silence as they waited for Jason Vickers to show.

The thin man came on the stroke of midnight, and Fisher suspected that he had been waiting nearby, timing his arrival to perfection. And dramatic effect.

Vickers rode out without speaking.

Lee pulled into the column in equal silence.

Jubal Farrow was the only man who spoke with him, and that was no more than a whispered "good luck".

They rode west again, crossing the river to head south of Lawrence, then swinging back towards Pottawatomie Creek. The moon was up to its full girth, pale light spilling over the countryside like a warning lantern.

Fisher wondered where they were headed.

South of the Pottawatomie they came on a hollow surrounded by trees. Twin ridges spread out to east and west, shading the area from the north wind, but letting sunlight in. The basin was no more than a half-mile across, the

111

bottomland taken up with crops. At the centre, where a stream fed water to the land, was a small cabin.

Vickers halted his riders on the ridge.

He called them in around him and began to speak.

"Man that owns that place is called Jethro Marsh. He's white. He's got a nigger woman he calls his wife. Even wed, according to him. They got two kids."

The riders murmured. It sounded angry to Fisher.

"Marsh says that blacks are equal to white folks. Deserve to be treated the same. He wants to put his coffee-coloured bastards into school alongside white children. What do you say?"

"Kill him," murmured the horsemen.

Then louder: "Kill him!"

"KILL HIM."

"KILL HIM!"

Vickers raised his arms for silence. It came fast.

"Sure we will. That's why we're here. Only don't no one touch Marsh. We're gonna hang him. Our new recruit is gonna hang him, I promise you."

The Jayhawkers spilled over the ridge in a solid wave, converging on the cabin with Vickers and James at their head. Fisher held back, wondering what to do.

He knew that he couldn't back out. Not without losing his cover; maybe even putting Emma in danger. So he went down with them, hoping that the people in the cabin might hear them coming and escape. If not that, then maybe someone else would kill them.

The door of the little hut opened and a woman showed. She was young, black and beautiful, a thin cotton shift tugged over her firm breasts.

A gun exploded flame across the darkness, and she staggered back, clutching at her shoulder. More shots echoed through the night and Fisher watched her face disintegrate, blood spilling thick and dark over her shift.

She tumbled back and a man took her place, clutching a single-barrel shotgun.

One of Vickers' riders screamed as the shot hit his chest and face. The man with the shotgun ran out on the porch, swinging his ancient gun like a club. He lifted one rider from his saddle, then fell back as another slapped a pistol barrel across his head.

Fisher dismounted as the men went inside. He drew his Colt and followed them.

Then wished he hadn't.

There were two children huddled back against the hand-built bed set into one side of the cabin. They were curly-haired and pale-faced, a boy and a girl. They were sitting up, eyes wide, and mouths open, looking scared at the ruckus.

Vickers' men shot them both.

An old woman, black as the coals glowing in the fire, ran at the raiders, waving a broom in hopeless defence. They shot her, too.

Then Vickers was in the room, flanked by Caleb James with his shotgun.

"Burn it," he said. "But take the man outside first."

Fisher holstered his pistol and followed the raiders out.

Two men were dragging Marsh away from the cabin. Inside, the fire was taking hold. Fisher couldn't be sure, but he thought that he could smell the obscenely sweet odour of roasting flesh. Human flesh.

He turned away, fighting the nausea tugging hard at his stomach.

Then Vickers broke the silence.

"Hang him," said the thin man. "Hang that bastard to prove you're with us."

8

THERE was a long silence, and Fisher took a deep breath.

The silence got broken by the sound of a rope dropping over a tree. Fisher looked towards the noise. A noose of good hemp was swinging from the branch of an old pine. The tree looked solid and aged, as though it had seen a lot happen in this sleepy hollow. The rope looked new and strong. As strong as the bough from which it hung.

Hung . . .

The word stuck in Fisher's mind.

Hung . . . Hung: Vickers was going to force him into hanging Jethro Marsh. And if he backed out, he would be dead.

Most likely, Emma, too.

He swung out of the saddle, looking towards Vickers.

"Get it done," said the thin man, his pale face splitting into a cadaverous smile. "Hang him."

Fisher glanced around. Twenty, maybe more,

men were watching him. Waiting. Like vultures, he thought. Like carrion eaters hungry for prey.

He moved towards Marsh.

That cold, uncompromising part of his mind that came into action when danger threatened was working at full pace. There was no way, no way at all, that he could back off from this killing. He had five shots in his pistol, one more in the Sharps buffalo gun sheathed along his saddle. Too few shots for the men watching him.

And if he tried to break away, Emma was in danger. McGarry too, perhaps.

A break—whatever the outcome—would boil the lid right off his cover story. Most likely leaving him dead with his body full of holes while the outlaws rode free.

There was only one way to go.

He had to hang Jethro Marsh.

"Sure," he said, walking towards the farmer. "Sure."

He hoped that his voice sounded normal.

He took the rope and set it over Marsh's head. The farmer was numb with shock and took the rope with seemingly casual ease, even turning his head over to the side so that it was easier to fit the hemp about his neck. Fisher pulled the noose tight, dragging the loop up against Marsh's neck.

Maybe that way the man would die fast; the rope might snap his spine, rather than strangling him.

He felt sweat break out on his hands and back. Then he hiked the farmer up on to the waiting horse. Someone had brought it out from the corral behind the homestead, a fat-bellied plough horse that stood quiet, oblivious to what was going on.

Marsh climbed astride the bare back like he didn't care.

Or didn't know.

Fisher stepped back.

The tail end of the rope was looped around the bole of the tree. The man on the horse was outlined against the ridge by the flames of his burning home. There was a sickly sweet smell of roasting flesh, overlayed by the thicker odour of smouldering timber.

Fisher drew his gun.

For a moment he thought about using it on Vickers and James. Then three more of the renegades But he knew it wouldn't work.

Couldn't work.

It was a dead end path.

Either way.

He thumbed back the hammer and backed off from the horse.

He squeezed the trigger, scorching a bullet along the plough horse's withers.

The horse jerked, lashing its hindquarters backwards against the sting of the shot. Then it took off, thundering away into the night.

Jethro Marsh was left dangling. The horse went out from under him and the rope dragged tight about his neck. The farmer made a noise. Fisher couldn't tell if it was a cry for help or a curse. Maybe it was just a noise.

Marsh dangled.

His face turned red, then purple as his tongue stuck out from between his wide-spread lips. A spray of excrement flooded through his night-shirt, staining the cloth. It dripped from his legs.

Fisher jumped back to avoid it.

Marsh made another noise.

It sounded like a curse, but it was difficult for Fisher to tell. Then the farmer swung limp. His tongue stuck out from his mouth, black; his head canted over to one side; his eyes stared at nothing.

He was dead.

Fisher turned towards Jonas Vickers. He fought down the impulse to draw his gun and use it. Instead he smiled.

"Well?" He hoped his voice wasn't too thick with disgust. "Did that convince you?"

Vickers laughed. It was a dry sound. Like wind rustling through sagebrush.

"Mount up, Lee. That was good enough for me."

Fisher climbed on to his horse. The black stallion sensed his nerves and got skittish, so he had to fight it to a standstill. Vickers turned to the waiting men.

"He's all right, boys! He's proved himself. Let's go home."

They rode away without a backward glance. The cabin was mostly burned down, the rank odour of human flesh overcome by the smell of the timber.

Marsh's body hung where it was left.

The memory stuck in Fisher's mind.

They got back to Independence in the early hours of dawn. The sun was beginning to glance bright shadows over the land, rimming the buildings with soft, golden light. It looked peaceful.

And Fisher felt sick.

He felt worse when he found that Emma wasn't there.

The room was empty, the bed neat and undisturbed. Fisher checked the bathroom, then went back to look for a note. There was no message and he felt a sudden pang of fear. Flicking open the lid of the watch tucked into his vest pocket, he checked the time: it was a little after three.

Cursing under his breath, Fisher hurried down the stairs.

The same clerk as before was snoring at the desk, his shoulders moving rhythmically in time with the sawing noise. Fisher shook him awake.

"What? Whassa matter?"

The clerk looked up, blearily, shaking his head as he forced himself to concentrate.

"Miss Wright," grated Fisher, "where is she?"

"I don't know," The clerk looked like he wanted to get back to sleep. "Didn't she tell you?"

Fisher reached over the desk, grabbing the lapels of the man's jacket with both hands. The clerk was yanked from his chair, dragged part way across the desk so that he found himself staring into dark eyes that sent a chill running fastdown his spine. He had guessed Fisher was dangerous the moment the tall man walked into the hotel. It was something to do with the way he moved: lazy-smooth, yet tensed, like a cat; something to do with the way his eyes took in a room, checking the people there while his right hand stayed close to his side, close to the bulge of the pistol under the black coat.

Suddenly the pistol was in Fisher's hand.

The hammer going back sounded unnaturally loud in the early morning quiet.

"I'll count to three," rasped Fisher. "Then I squeeze the trigger." He held the clerk with his left hand, resting the muzzle of the Navy Colt on the bridge of the man's nose. The clerk went cross-eyed and his teeth began to chatter.

"I don't know! I swear I don't!"

"One," said Fisher.

"Christ!" gasped the clerk. "You can't kill me."

"Yes I can," said Fisher calmly. "Two."

"She didn't leave no message," wailed the clerk, his voice throaty with fear. "She just called fer that rig you hired an' took off."

"Which direction?" asked Fisher.

"Jesus, mister. I don't know. Headed east, I think."

"What time?"

"Round midnight." The clerk fought down an urgent need to urinate. "Soon after you left."

Fisher let hold of his collar and the man slumped over the desk, eyes still fixed on the gun. He felt something warm run down his leg and blushed: it was a long time since he'd wet himself in sheer terror.

"If she comes back, tell her to stay put," ordered Fisher. "Tell her to wait for me."

"Yessir. I'll do that." The clerk watched Fisher leave, a long sigh escaping from his lips as the black-suited man went through the door. "Bastard."

The last word was very quiet, pitched low so that Fisher wouldn't hear.

He wouldn't have cared if he had. There was too much on his mind for him to worry about one insignificant hotel clerk.

"Bastard," repeated the man, louder this time. "Damn' gun-happy bastard killer."

He settled back across the desk, composing an edited version of the story. It would make good telling when he met up with Joe and the others, how he was threatened by a wild-eyed gunman and backed the man down. Yeah, when Lee Fisher pulled a gun on Nathan Webster he hadn't counted on facing a man prepared to risk his life in defence of the hotel, and he'd run like a scared coyote. Pistol an' all.

Nathan went back to sleep, satisfied with his role as hero.

Fisher ran to the stable. There had been something Emma said that could be a lead. What the hell was it? *If I saw Beaumont alone . . . He might talk to a woman he was planning to seduce . . .* Something like that. It was all he had, and a low pair is better than a dead hand.

He went through the side door of the big barn at a run. The Negro who slept in the loft was just finishing rubbing down the black stallion, and gaped in amazement as Fisher threw blanket and saddle over the big horse's back.

"I changed my mind," grunted Fisher, ramming a knee into the animal's belly to tighten the girth strap.

He hooked a foot into the stirrup and mounted. The Negro ran to open the main gate, then jumped back as Fisher thundered past.

Emma had felt angry as Lee left. She was tired of being treated like some inferior species, too helpless to look after herself. It was the thing she disliked most about Lee Fisher: his arrogant assumption that a woman was a useless hindrance to his work. She had made up her mind to prove him wrong in the only way that seemed open. Her idea about seeing Beaumont was sound—every female instinct she had told her that. So she decided to see the plump Southern gentleman. She would weadle information from him in return for a promise of bed. And if Beaumont tried to collect on the promise, she had the derringer in her bag and the second little gun holstered on her thigh.

And for a while it all went according to her plan.

Beaumont was drinking brandy when she arrived, his plump features even more flushed than usual. He was surprised to see her, but did his best to hide it beneath a mask of sophistication.

"A most pleasant surprise, Emma. You'll have a drink with me, I trust?"

125

Emma nodded, smiling. She had selected a dark green dress for the occasion, one that nipped in her waist, emphasising the curving line of her hips, and cut low at the front so that her breasts were pushed up and forwards. She had taken pains with her make-up, adding just a little too much colour to her lips and shading her green eyes with seductive shadowing. She played the part of the bored mistress.

"I hope you'll forgive me, Charles. I know I shouldn't be here at this hour, but I hate waiting around that hotel for Lee to get back. I felt so desperate for company I just climbed in the buggy and came to you."

Beaumont passed her a glass. Emma noticed it was filled higher than usual.

"And where is Lee? I'd not have thought he would leave anyone as pretty as you."

Emma simpered. "Why, Charles! You do say the sweetest things. And you know full well where Lee is. It was you sent him to see that Jonas Vickers, wasn't it?"

Beaumont smiled carelessly. "Well, yes. But I'm not sure . . ."

"Come now," said Emma, settling herself on a chair so that the fat man would get a better view of her cleavage. "You know everything that goes on around here. I know what Lee's doing, and I know that you do, too. After all, Lee and Vickers, the others, they're just—well—soldiers, aren't they? You're the commander."

Beaumont hiked his shoulders back, trying hard to suck in the swell of his gut. It was a useless effort and he gave it up in favour of a chair, leaning over to put his face close to Emma's.

"You might say that, my dear. In a way I am."

"I know you are," said Emma, smiling still. "You're the one with the money. The others do what you tell them, don't they?"

Beaumont smiled. He sensed a sudden change of allegiance: this lovely woman was as mercenary as the rest. He entertained no great vanity about his looks, knew that he drank too much and was too fond of his food to compete with someone like Fisher. But he had money. And that was a factor that he used to his advantage, just as he used his privileged contacts with the important people in the South.

"Perhaps," he said. "I'm not sure I should say."

"Come now," Emma murmured, leaning

towards him. "I admire a man who knows how to run things. Anyone can pull a trigger. It takes brains to make it profitable."

Beaumont reached for the decanter, topping their glasses.

"Doesn't Lee have brains?" he asked. "He struck me as a shrewd man."

Emma pouted, conscious of the effect it had on Beaumont.

"Lee is good-looking, but that's not everything," she said. "We met in St. Louis, and I thought he could—what can I say?—look after me. But he spends his time gambling or riding off with your friend Jonas. I like to be taken out, not left alone in some dreary hotel."

"I can understand your problem." Beaumont was getting a glitter in his eyes that wasn't entirely due to the brandy. "You're a woman who should be looked after. I certainly looked, the first time we met."

He chuckled at his joke and emptied his glass.

"That's what I mean," said Emma. "You're the kind of man who knows how to treat a lady."

Beaumont took a deep breath. This was going even better than he had hoped. This woman

128

obviously wanted some kind of security, the kind that money bought. Well, Charles Fremantle Beaumont had money, and just now he was without a mistress. The coloured girls Vickers brought him were fine for a while, fine for a little fun, but it would be pleasant to have a mistress he could take out in public, maybe even to St. Louis or New Orleans. Yes, heads would turn then, when they saw Charles F. Beaumont riding by with Emma Wright in his carriage.

He glanced down at her breasts, pretending to study his glass. They were young and firm —she couldn't be much over twenty—and that hair! Beaumont decided to stake his cards.

"Perhaps," he said quietly, "we might explore the situation. I do get lonely in this house, on my own."

Emma smiled, encouraging him. "What are you saying?"

"That you might like to . . . uh . . . choose to live . . . elsewhere?"

"Why Charles!" Emma pretended embarrassment. "Are you suggesting I should come live with you?"

"Why not?" Beaumont decided to forget

129

caution. Until he remembered Fisher's lean face. "Though Lee might be a problem."

"Yes," said Emma. "He's the jealous kind. But I'm sure you can handle him."

"I'm no gunfighter," said Beaumont quickly. "Perhaps I can buy him off."

"Oh, shoo." Emma thrust her cleavage at the fat man. "I'm sure you can handle Lee. Why, you're on the same side, aren't you? I'll bet you have papers that say you're the boss here."

"Well," Beaumont sounded cautious so Emma took a deep breath and leaned closer still, "I do have some documents . . ."

"Can I see them?" Emma pouted again. "Lee never tells me anything."

"They're in the safe box," said Beaumont, staring hard at her expanded breasts. "In my bedroom."

"May I see them?" Emma made her voice husky. "Please, Charles? Just so I'm sure you can handle Lee."

"Why not come with me?" said Beaumont. "We can look at them upstairs."

Emma simpered some more. "No, Charles. A lady has to protect her reputation. You might just be saying that to get me in your bedroom, and then where would I be? You bring them down and prove you can look after me. Then we'll see."

Beaumont came out of his chair like a buck rabbit with a hound nipping at its heels. Emma watched him go, congratulating herself on the success of her mission. The fat man went through the doors like a racehorse slamming out of the gates, pausing long enough to dismiss the two manservants waiting in the hall before plunging up the stairs.

When he returned, he carried a thin sheaf of documents.

"Look at those." He dropped the papers in Emma's lap, preening. "They should convince you."

Emma picked up the topmost paper.

It was a letter, written on plain parchment, in a flowing hand.

Dear Charles, *it began*, I know that you are doing your utmost to further our cause in Missouri and Kansas, and I thank you most sincerely for your efforts. It must be hard for you, living so close to those tiresome farmers who insist on maintaining the sad myth of Negro equality. You have my honest thanks, and my sympathy, for what you do may well effect the outcome of the world. There is a storm brewing, Charles, a storm that will turn the tide of the future; and you are part of that storm. I am sending someone to help you. He is a good man, devoted to our cause and much trusted by me, and those about me. His name is Jonas Vickers. He will make himself known by the password: The South is Free. Trust him, Charles. He will aid you greatly.

It was signed, Jonathan Ridley.

"Who's Jonathan Ridley?" asked Emma.

Beaumont smiled, pleasured by his "secret" information. "If war breaks out, Jonathan will head the intelligence forces. He's my cousin."

Emma smiled some more and turned the other letters. There were several more documents from men she had never heard of, someone called Jackson, a man who signed himself Wm. Quantril. They added up to a massive indictment against Beaumont, sufficient to guarantee the fat man's hanging, along with Jonas Vickers and Caleb James, and the rest.

"Well," she said, handing the papers back to Beaumont, "you really are someone important."

Beaumont was three-quarters through the

brandy bottle, his face looking like a near-cooked lobster. His breath came in short, sharp gasps as he stared at her.

"Exactly," he said. "I'm someone. Someone to reckon with. If Fisher doesn't like it, he can go argue with the people who're going to run this country. Does that make up your mind?"

"Maybe." Emma smiled, easing her way up from the chair. "I'll have to think about it."

"Think about it?" Beaumont's voice contained a edge of hysteria. "Isn't that enough? Stay here. Stay with me."

He moved across to stand above her, close enough that his belly blocked off her escape. To stand up, she needed to shove him aside.

"I need some time," she murmured, reaching for her bag.

"Let me give you my answer tomorrow."

Beaumont reached down, snatching the bag from her hand. He tossed it across the room.

"Stay," he gasped. And threw his bulk over her.

Emma tried to fight him off, but his weight pinned her to the chair, trapping her arms as he drove his face against her neck and lips. She panicked as his hands clutched at her dress, fumbling for the hooks fastening the material down her back. There was a tearing sound and she felt the dress rip, the fastenings torn away. Beaumont used both hands to drag the garment over her shoulders, yanking it down her arms so that she was caught even when he leaned back.

He jerked the dress clear of her breasts. His lips were wet, and his eyes shone bright with lust.

"Stay with me," he mumbled. "Stay with me. I need you."

Emma swung an arm at his head, but he caught her wrist, twisting it back. He pinned her against the chair, using both his weight and his strength to hold her still as he fumbled beneath her skirts.

She screamed. And Beaumont laughed.

"There's no one," he panted. "Only us. Don't worry, Emma. Darling. I'll give you everything."

He reached down, fumbling at his belt. Emma struck at his face, trying to rake her nails down his cheek, but he turned his head aside, nuzzling at her breasts. He used his free hand to rip at her undergarments. The cotton tore and Emma felt the material tug at her back, felt the sting of whalebone drawn tight over her spine and ribs. Then felt it break as her breasts spilled free.

Beaumont reached up, trapping her left arm, and buried his face against her body.

She screamed, then felt the cry cut off by Beaumont's mouth. His lips were wet and hot, his tongue probing. Emma gagged, trying to bite his tongue.

He drew back, releasing her left arm. For a fat man he moved fast. Before she could strike at him he swung his arm back and round again, palm open so that the slap thudded heavy against her cheek. It smashed her head sideways and she tasted blood as her teeth snapped on the side of her tongue.

The hand shifted back. Once. Twice. Three times, like a metronome, or the pendulum of a clock. Emma tried to reach the tiny Remington-Elliott derringer tucked into her garter, but her head was spinning and Beaumont's grip was too strong. She fell back. And felt the whole front of her dress rip away. Felt the sudden tug of her underclothes, and the rush of air against her exposed body.

Beaumont whined like a dog in heat, burying his face against her neck as he pushed towards her.

She felt something that was warm and hard shove between her thighs. Tried to close her legs.

The man's knees forced her apart. His breath was hot and heavy with brandy fumes on her face. She tried to butt her forehead against his nose, but he turned his face aside, biting on her shoulder.

There was a tearing sound and she realised that her petticoats were gone.

Beaumont eased back, tugging at his belt. His trousers fell away, drooping about his feet. He reached down, snapping the buttons that closed his underwear, grinning lasciviously as his belly and legs became exposed.

He hit her again as she reached for the gun on her thigh, rocking her head back against the chair. She felt powerful hands take hold of her wrists, spreading her arms wide; the thrust of a body between her legs, spreading them even as a florid, suffused face crushed against hers.

Lord! No! she thought as Beaumont thrust towards her. Not like this. Please! Not like this.

Dimly, as though through a veil of horror and pain, she heard the sound of breaking glass.

The staccato, far-distant, reverberation of a gun.

A warm stickiness oozed over her inner thighs, the faint memory of a scream echoed in her mind.

And she looked up at Lee Fisher, smoke floating lazily from the barrel of the Colt's Navy pistol in his right hand.

9

BEAUMONT'S head tilted sideways. There was a jagged hole in the left temple, blood oozing thickly down the fat cheek. Fisher grabbed the corpse and hauled it clear, glancing in surprised appreciation at Emma's near-naked body.

"Looks like I arrived just in time," he said softly.

"You might have killed *me*." Emma tugged her tattered dress about her.

Fisher shook his head. "I'm too good a shot."

Emma started to say something else, but he waved her silent, glancing at the papers scattered over the carpet.

"Listen, we'll have to work fast. There'll be servants coming soon and I can't afford to be linked with this. Tell them you never saw the man who did it, that way Vickers might think it was a Northern sympathiser. Can you handle that?"

Emma nodded, staring at Beaumont. The blood was staining an expensive carpet, matting the thick pile with a growing circle of dark maroon.

"And give me those guns."

She let her dress fall apart, handing him the derringer. He stepped across to take the other from her bag. There was a pounding on the doors, and he ducked back through the shattered windows.

Emma drew her torn dress over her body again and took a deep breath. "Come in," she called.

The marshal was still talking with Emma when Vickers sent for Lee. The dark man had got back to Independence without being spotted, and felt that a two-dollar handout should seal up the Negro stablehand's mouth. The hotel clerk was another problem; one that got solved with five dollars and discreet reference to Samuel Colt's excellent products.

Waiting for the results was the worst part for Fisher. He settled down to sleep—in the bed, for the first time—and got woken by a vaguely familiar voice shouting through the door. When he opened it, he saw Matt Granger waiting for him.

"You heard what happened?" The reporter was boiling over with excitement.

Fisher shook his head.

"Charles Beaumont got shot! Someone put a bullet right through the man's skull. Marshal Ellis has your ladyfriend in his office now. Seems like she was there when it happened. Did you know?"

"No," grunted Fisher, "I didn't."

Granger looked surprised. "You got any comment to make?"

"Yeah," said Fisher. "You woke me up. I need coffee, an' I've obviously got things to do. If you want to talk, do it tonight."

He shut the door and punched the service bell. The coffee came along with hot water, carried by the same nervous porter. Fisher shaved and dressed in between swallows of coffee. He felt tired and irritable and ready to play his part as he left the hotel for the town jail.

Marshal Ellis was all tactful understanding.

He knew that Mr. Fisher and Miss Wright were Southern friends of Mr. Beaumont; more important—it seemed—they were friends of Mr. Vickers. Talking with Miss Wright was little more than a formality: it was obvious that

140

she couldn't have killed Mr. Beaumont. But the marshal had to keep up appearances, even though he needed to file a report for the US Marshal. But they need not worry about that. Marshal Harlan was a friend; a sympathetic friend, if Mr. Fisher knew what he meant.

Lee reminded himself to mention Ellis to the Chief when they reported back to St. Louis.

Then Vickers' message arrived and the lawman let them both go. Lee escorted Emma back to the Creole Palace and went directly to Vickers in the Lost Dog saloon.

The pale man was angry as all hell.

"You kill him?"

"No. Why the hell would you think that?"

"Your woman was with him. Why? What the devil was she doing there?"

Fisher shrugged. "She got bored. She's a lady with an eye for money. I've sorted that out with her. She never saw the man."

"I know what she said." Vickers' fingers drummed angrily on the table. "I don't like it."

"Nor do I," said Fisher. "I let her know that. She won't try the same thing again."

"And she saw nothing?" Vickers sounded doubtful. "Nothing at all?"

"Jesus!" Fisher shouted. "Don't you think I

141

asked her? You think I like this? Beaumont damn' near raped her. Whoever it was shot the fat bastard, saved her."

Vickers looked at him. It was an unpleasant scrutiny, and Fisher hoped that he retained his character of the wronged lover. Thinking about Emma and Beaumont, it wasn't too hard a part to play.

"Get rid of her," rasped the thin man. "The sooner the better."

"Why?" protested Fisher. "I can keep her in line from now on. She won't make any more trouble."

"Lose her," snarled Vickers. "I don't give a damn' how, but lose her. There's too much talk coming from last night, and we can't afford it. Not with what's coming up."

Fisher bought time by walking over to the table and lifting the decanter. He raised the cut glass in Vickers' direction, questioning. Vickers shook his head and Lee poured himself a stiff measure of whisky.

"All right," he said evenly, "I'll get rid of her. What's coming up? The raid you talked about? Where I play lynch pin?"

Vickers paused for a moment, thinking. He stared out of the window, watching the traffic of Independence go by. Then he turned back to face Lee, his skull-like face more sombre than ever.

"Yeah. The big one's coming up faster than I wanted now that Beaumont's dead, and I need you for that."

He broke off, staring at Fisher. It was though he assessed his options, weighing doubts against past performance. Lee sipped his whisky, hoping that his face was straight, that he looked and acted the part of Southern renegade. Finally, Vickers broke the silence.

"We're heading into a war between North and South. It's not declared yet, but it's been brewing for a long time, and it's coming soon. What we need to do is capitalise on it: there's money to be made out of a war. The men who grab the right parcels at the beginning of the game are the ones who end up with the most at the finish. That sound right to you?"

Fisher nodded.

"Good," said Vickers, "I thought you'd agree. Fact is, there's a Northern sympathiser called Wilde. Robert Wilde. He's a big man in Kansas, owns a whole lot of land. Cattle, farms, business interests, that kind of thing. We've been raiding him a lot. Kind of warning him off. But he hasn't taken the warnings. That means we have to hit him in the gut. Where it really hurts."

He waved a hand towards the bottles, motioning for Fisher to pour him a drink. Lee filled a glass and passed it over the table.

"Thanks," said Vickers. "Fact is that Wilde is the centre of Northern interests in Kansas. If we can destroy him, the other land owners will most likely swing to the South. So I plan to wipe him out."

"How?" asked Fisher, genuinely interested.

Vickers smiled. It looked bad.

"He lives in a township called Northville. Owns the bank there and most of the country around. I want to take it all away from him. If we can do that, we take the backbone out of the yankees in Kansas."

"Sounds good," urged Fisher. "But how?"

"You," said Vickers. "Wilde won't know yet how you think on the issue. That's why you're the lynch pin. I want you to ride in there and kill him."

Fisher played his part: "How do I handle it?"

"He doesn't know you," said Vickers, "and I heard he was hiring help. I don't know from where, but that doesn't matter. You go in as a hired gun looking for work. Get yourself a job as his bodyguard, something like that. Just get close enough to kill him. I'll have a man waiting outside of town so you'll have a link with me. Let him know when you reckon to kill Wilde and I'll bring our people in the same day. We take over the town."

Fisher smiled, nodding. Vickers' thinking was falling right into line with his own—all the way to an ambush.

"When do I leave?" he asked.

"Get rid of the woman first," said Vickers in that dust-dry voice. "Then stay around a while until I've got everyone ready. Let's say you leave next week sometime."

"Right. That makes sense."

Fisher left the saloon feeling more cheerful than when he walked in. At least Vickers didn't suspect him. Back at the hotel he returned Emma's guns and explained the situation. They agreed that she should quit Independence as soon as possible, taking a boat west along the Kansas river as far as Lawrence. From there she could wire a full report back to St. Louis and outline the situation to McGarry, who by then should be waiting in Lawrence for word from Fisher.

Given that advance warning, Brad should be able to set up a trap of some kind before Lee arrived in Northville. After that it would be a question of waiting for Vickers to put his head in the noose.

At least, that was the way Fisher hoped it would happen.

There wasn't a lot else he could do, anyway.

There was a boat leaving the next morning and Fisher booked Emma a berth. The way Fisher had it worked out, Emma could warn McGarry of the coming attack giving him time to organise some kind of defence. Then, when Lee got to Northville, they could work out a detailed plan for an ambush.

If it all went the way Fisher hoped, they would wipe out Vickers and his raiders in one blow. And whatever the outcome, he was pleased that Emma would be safely out of the way.

He watched the boat head upstream, then turned away, walking back to the bustling centre of Independence. He went to the stable and settled up for the buggy: with Emma gone he wouldn't be needing the gentleman's carriage. After that, he visited the second stable and bought the black horse. With full rig, the animal cost him seventy dollars. Idly, he wondered if the Chief would object to footing the bill when he saw the expense chit. He guessed not; at least, not if his plan worked out. And if it didn't, the chances were he wouldn't be around to argue the point.

Grinning to himself, he made his way back to the hotel. It felt good to be heading into direct action again.

Back at the Creole Palace heads turned as he entered the dining-room. Fisher ignored the curious stares along with the buzz of conversation, taking his usual table with a calm indifference that sparked off a fresh wave of speculation. He ate in silence and spent the afternoon in his room, feeling bored. In the evening he went to the Lost Dog and played cards. He won thirty dollars.

The next few days passed in similar fashion and he began to feel bored. Vickers stayed out of sight, and Fisher left it that way: there was no point in pushing his luck. McGarry would need time to get back to Northville and set things up at that end, so Lee would have to fill his time as best he could.

Cards helped. And a sloe-eyed girl who reminded him of another saloon hostess he had met. That had been what felt like a lifetime ago in a nowhere town called Wheeler. There was no particular reason to think about the girl, but she had stuck in his mind. Maybe because she had been an orphan, too, a drifter like him, wandering from town to town, riding the long downhill slope towards some dirty cantina and flea-ridden back room somewhere at fifty cents a throw. He wondered where she was now, then pushed the thought away. Dammit! He was getting sentimental as he got older.

After a week he was ready to show his hand, push Vickers into making a move. But the thin man forestalled him.

Caleb James entered the saloon as Fisher emptied his third glass, elbowing his way over to the bar.

Fisher pushed the bottle across. "Drink?"

"Thanks," grunted James, helping himself. "The Captain wants to see you."

"It's about time," said Fisher. "I've got a bellyful of doing nothing."

"Yeah, I'll bet," chuckled James. "With that woman o' yores gone I guess you ain't got much to do."

Fisher ignored the clumsy humour, reminding himself that he was supposed to be on the same side as the bearded man.

"When?" he asked.

"Right now. Upstairs."

Fisher emptied his glass and tossed a coin on the bar. He led the way up to Vickers' room and knocked on the door.

Vickers called for him to enter and he stepped inside. The renegade was leafing through some papers that he tucked into a scroll-worked bureau before Fisher could see them. He locked the drawer and looked up, his angular face sombre.

"There's a change of plan."

Apprehension sent nervous warnings tingling down Fisher's spine.

"What change?" he asked, worried.

"I just got word from friends in St. Louis," said Vickers slowly. "It seems like Wilde hired himself some damn' detective agency to investigate the raids. I don't know the exact details, but there's an agent in Northville right now. And two more were sent. A man and a woman."

Fisher did his best to look casual and interested at the same time. He shrugged, moving into the room so that he could cross over to the far wall. Caleb James moved faster.

The big man looked as though he was headed for the whisky, and the way he got behind Lee might have been accidental. Until Fisher remembered that James never took a drink without Vickers inviting him.

He turned slightly, putting himself in a position where he could see both men.

"So?" he said. "We'd best move fast."

"Yeah." Vickers nodded. "That's what I was thinking. Trouble is, I don't like the idea of riding into a trap."

"How can we?" Fisher spread his hands, letting them fall close to his hips. "There's no one but us knows about the plan."

"Exactly." Vickers' voice was exceptionally quiet. Fisher was reminded of a wind rustling leaves in a graveyard. "No one but us."

"Hold it!" Fisher faked anger. "You don't think that I'm a spy."

There was a long silence as Vickers stared at him, something almost like a smile stretching his narrow lips.

"You're a stranger," he murmured. "All we know about you is what you told us, and that's not a whole lot. You came here with a woman."

"Dammit!" snarled Fisher. "She's gone now."

"Yeah," said Vickers. "Gone to Lawrence. It's only two, maybe three days, from there to Northville. That'd give her a clear week to tell your partner what's going on. Long enough for him to set up a trap."

"Christ!" Fisher put his hands on his hips, shoving back the tails of his coat. "I proved myself, didn't I? Twice, dammit!"

"Your woman was with Beaumont when he was shot." Vickers ignored Lee's anger. "Where were you?"

"With you," shouted Fisher. "With you on that raid. I was hanging a man."

"Sure you were." Vickers' tone was mild. "But you got back here in plenty of time to ride out and shoot the fat man. I wouldn't blame you for that. It's the rest I don't like."

"I was in my room," grunted Fisher. "That newspaperman, Granger, saw me there."

"In the morning." Vickers smiled again. "You were gone most of the night."

"Yeah?" grated Fisher. "What proof you got? Who says I wasn't there?"

"He does."

Vickers pointed over his shoulder at the

151

bedroom. The door swung open and three men stepped out. Two were standing, holding the third between them. Fisher recognised them as members of the gang. The other man had his head down, slumped on his chest. There was blood showing through his thinning hair. Vickers reached out, tugging the man's face into view. The nose was broken, twisted over at an angle, and the lips were thick and bloody where fists had pounded. Both eyes were puffed closed and burns showed, dark and ugly, on the cheeks. It was hard to recognise the desk clerk from the Creole Palace.

"Who's he?" said Fisher.

Vickers let the head drop back. "You don't know him?"

"Should I?"

"He works the night desk at your hotel. Starts at eight, finishes at seven. He says you came in late and went out again. After you asked about the woman. Then you got back just before he went off duty. He says you paid him five dollars to keep his mouth shut."

"He's lying," said Fisher, letting his right hand slide closer to his gun. "He's a damn' liar."

"No," said Vickers softly. "You're the liar."

It was a long chance, but the only one Fisher had. He reached for the Navy Colt. Vickers first. Then Caleb James. Then—if he was lucky —the other two.

His hand closed on the butt. The gun slid up from the greased leather of the holster. Then something clamped down over his arms and he felt himself lifted off his feet. Vickers' Colt seemed to jump into his hand and the others let the clerk fall as they hauled pistols into sight.

Fisher cursed, kicking back. He heard James grunt with pain as his heels ground on to the big man's feet, then Vickers was in front of him, his arm swinging back. It arched forwards and Lee turned his head aside, trying to avoid the blow. The barrel of the Colt landed along his cheek and he tasted blood as his teeth jarred together. It swung back. Once. Twice . . .

Coloured lights exploded across his vision and he felt his stomach churn as his eyes went dim. Faintly, he was aware of James' arms releasing him so that he crumpled to the floor. Then there were only boots and pain exploding through his chest and back and belly.

10

McGARRY was furious when Emma told him what had happened. He could see no reason for Emma to risk her cover—or her life—in some wildbrained attempt at seduction. He saw less reason for killing Beaumont. Knock the man out, sure. That would have been enough; and safer. But kill him? Dammit all to hell, couldn't Lee Fisher keep his itchy trigger finger away from his gun long enough to think things through? With Beaumont shot dead while Emma lay around half-naked, the outlaws couldn't help but wonder about Fisher.

The only good thing to come out of the whole half-baked mess was Emma's escape. She argued against being left in Lawrence while Brad rode back to Northville, but he pulled rank to convince her that one of them had to stay in the clear to report back to St. Louis. It was the best he could do in the circumstances. With the raiders planning an all-out attack on the town he needed time to organise the defence. If Fisher got out of Independence in one piece, then good: his gun would be useful. If not—hell, Lee had only himself to blame.

McGarry sent word north to Fort Kearney. He doubted the Army could reach Northville in time, even if the fort could spare enough men, but a long shot was worth trying if you didn't have too many alternatives. Wilde was out of town, gone south to Fort Supply to discuss a grain contract with the Army, and had most of his men with him. It left Northville stripped pretty bare of useful guns.

McGarry counted the miles off by thinking up new ways to curse Fisher.

Lee was surprised that he wasn't dead.

He came to with a pain that felt like it began in his feet and burned its way up through his body into his brain. He was dimly conscious of straw prickling against his face and when he opened his eyes he realised he was stretched facedown, on what felt like a stable floor. One eye refused to open properly, and when he tried to spit some blood from his mouth a broken tooth fell out.

He lay still, trying to assess the extent of his injuries. His ribs felt like they were on fire, and his breath came in short, agonising gasps. He eased his head to the side, trying to locate himself.

It was difficult to be sure, but he thought he was in a barn or a stable. There were voices sounding off behind him, but he could not see the speakers without turning over. And right then turning over demanded more effort than he could muster. Instead, he peered ahead. There was a wall of old, broken planks, sunlight showing through and birdsong echoing from outside. Over to his left, he made out the shapes of long tables, something that looked like machinery. Suddenly he realised where he was: the old lumber mill. Vickers must have had him taken there from the saloon, leaving someone—two men to judge by the sound—to guard him.

He stayed quiet, wondering if he was too badly mauled to handle two men. The way he felt, he didn't have much of a chance; but there was only one way to find out.

He eased his arms up, pushing over on to his back.

The guards failed to hear him, their attention occupied by a game of stud. Fisher recognised one of them as Jubal Farrow. The other man he didn't know. Cautiously, he looked around. The mill was empty, only the three of them inside. Hell, he thought, it could be worse. He wasn't sure how, but it cheered him some.

He saw a piece of metal, part-hidden under the straw, and reached for it. His fingers closed on a length of broken saw blade, a six-inch sliver of metal, jagged and sharp where it had snapped. He drew it to him, tucking it under his jacket.

Then he let go a low moan.

At first they didn't hear him, so he repeated the cry, louder this time. Both men turned.

"Water," mumbled Fisher.

Farrow stood up. "The bastard's awake. Maybe we should tie him."

"What the hell for? The way Caleb worked him over, he ain't goin' nowhere. Give him some water. He won't be drinkin' too much more."

Grumbling, Farrow lifted a canteen and walked towards Fisher.

Lee's grip tightened on the rusty metal.

"Here, yankee." Farrow uncorked the canteen. "Take a drink."

Fisher moaned some more, reaching feebly with his left hand. He emphasised his weakness, holding his right arm close to his body as though the limb was broken. It wasn't difficult to play hurt.

"Water," he groaned. "Please. Water . . ."

His voice sounded thick, slurred even to him. To Farrow it must have sounded even weaker, because the weasel-faced man dropped to one knee, holding out the canteen to touch Fisher's lips.

Fisher raised his left hand some more. Just enough to touch the leather flask. As though desperate for a drink, he pulled the canteen closer, stretching Farrow off balance. He raised his head, sucking on the spout.

Then closed his hand on Farrow's wrist, jerking the man towards him.

Farrow toppled as Lee's right arm lifted up and round. The length of broken saw blade slammed into his stomach and he gulped, a look of blank surprise appearing on his face.

Lee groaned—in genuine pain—as the weight fell across his midriff. He left the steel shard buried in Farrow's gut as he reached down for the Colt's Dragoon on the man's left hip. His fingers were slippery with blood and the gun was heavier than his own Navy Colt, but he drew the pistol and cocked it while the second guard was still climbing to his feet, mouth opening in amazement.

The man's gun was clear of the holster when Fisher shot him. The angle was difficult, Farrow's writhing weight partially blocking his aim. But Lee Fisher was too good a pistoleer to miss. The bullet caught the man in his right shoulder, slamming him back as he twisted sideways under the impact. He dropped his gun, stumbling against the low table. Cards fluttered through the dusty air as the table overturned and the man lost his balance. Fisher shot him again. Through the chest. The guard fell back coughing blood. He tried to sit up but his eyes glazed before he was fully upright and he grunted and slumped over.

Fisher shoved Jubal Farrow away and dragged the second pistol from the man's belt. He was pleased to see that it was his own Colt's Navy model and dropped it in the holster still belted to his waist. Farrow was moaning, both hands clasped over his stomach. The broken saw was sunk in deep enough that only an inch of blood-greased metal protruded and the front of the outlaw's shirt was staining a darker shade of maroon.

Fisher pushed to his knees and rolled Farrow over.

"Where's Vickers?"

"Oh, Christ! You've killed me."

"Where's Vickers?" repeated Fisher. "Has he gone to Northville?"

Farrow went on groaning, his face unnaturally pale.

"Listen," said Fisher, turning the man's face so that he stared into Farrow's eyes, "I can help you. Tell me where Vickers has gone and I'll help you."

"Jesus!" whined Farrow. "I need a doctor."

"Where's Vickers?"

"He's leavin' tonight." Fisher had to bend down to hear. "The whole gang's been called in. Twelve, maybe fifteen, men. Now get me some help."

"Sure," said Fisher.

And set the Dragoon to Farrow's temple.

When he stood up he had to pause and fight for his balance. After a while the nausea passed and only the pain was left. He checked himself over, cursing when he saw the blood speckling his shirt and waistcoat. So far as he could tell, there was nothing broken. His ribs and stomach were badly bruised, and he thought that a couple of ribs might be cracked, but he could move. Stiffly. His arms and legs were sound, and his hands seemed to have missed Caleb James' attention. His face felt raw, but he could see quite well even with one eye half-shut, and his nose was intact.

He went looking for a horse.

Outside he found the black stallion, and his flat-brimmed hat slung on the saddlehorn. He brushed his hair back, conscious of clotted blood under his fingers, and set the stetson on his head. Then he climbed into the saddle and turned the big horse to the southwest.

Northville was three days' ride away and he had something like four hours' start on Vickers. He hoped he could make it.

Bradford McGarry was still waiting for Lee to show. Waiting and angry. Wilde wasn't due back with his men for ten days, and the good people of Northville had given up.

When McGarry put the word around they called a town meeting. Forty citizens had voted to pull stakes and wait out the trouble in other towns; most of the others had laughed at the idea, or voted to let the raiders in without opposition. After all, they claimed, it couldn't change much. The saloons and hotels would go on working: what good was a dead town to the South? The preacher offered to talk with Vickers and the few of Wilde's men still left decided to ride south to warn their boss. McGarry was on his own.

Common sense told him to pull out. If the information Emma had given him was correct, Vickers would take over the town without resistance, and he doubted it would take long for someone to tell the outlaw who he was. Staying was suicidal. He knew that. He knew, too, that he had undertaken a contract with Robert Wilde on behalf of the Agency. And Brad McGarry had a powerful sense of duty. He decided to stay there and see what he could do.

He already had a good vantage point picked out. A flat-roofed building halfway down the main street. If he left his horse behind the building there was a narrow chance that he could pick off a few raiders and still get away. There was a chance that Wilde would get back early and rouse his neighbours to defend themselves. There was a chance that Fort Kearney would send troops down in time.

McGarry didn't stake too much hope on any of the chances.

But he still had a sense of duty.

Lee Fisher had three senses as he pushed the black horse west at a killing pace.

The first was purely physical: pain. He had to concentrate to stay in the saddle, gritting his teeth against the shafts of agony lancing through his body as the animal's hooves pounded ground. The second was of hate and raw anger. A burning desire to forestall Jonas Vickers and kill him. Any damn' way he could, no matter what the cost. The third was one McGarry would have applauded: Lee wanted to reach Northville ahead of the raiders and warn his partner.

Those last two fought the first and kept him in the saddle for most of the night. Around dawn he pulled the black horse to a stop and climbed down. His legs were shaky and it was about all he could do to water the horse and hobble it before collapsing on to a bed of pine needles and letting his eyes close.

He slept like a dead man, though some part of his mind stayed alert enough to wake him a few hours later, stiff and shivering in the early morning cold.

It was a bright morning, the sun rising hot and yellow over the pines. The Missouri river was behind him, Kansas stretching ahead. He was hungry and hurting still, and wished that he had time to start a fire, boil up some water for a shave and to cook breakfast. But he had neither time or food, so he climbed back into the saddle and urged the black up to a mile-eating canter. Thinking back to the maps he had seen in St. Louis he guessed he had two more days on the trail before hitting Northville. Maybe, somewhere along the line, he would find a homestead where he could buy food.

Close on noon he found a cabin tucked into the southern face of a sun-dappled hollow. The ground around had been cleared, and hogs were rooting amongst the stumps of trees.

There was a stream flowing through the meadow fronting the little house, and smoke rose lazily from the chimney.

Fisher rode down with both hands in clear view and reined in on the near side of the stream.

He shouted across and after a while a man

appeared in the door. He had a long-barrelled rifle aimed at Fisher's chest.

"State yore business, mister."

He sounded nervous.

"I need food," called Lee. "Grain for the horse, too. I can pay for both."

The man looked past him, studying the slopes. The rifle stayed pointed at his body. Then, satisfied that he was alone, the farmer waved him in. He started to ask where Fisher was headed until he saw the bruises, then changed his question to a worried concern about Fisher's injuries.

Fisher made up a story about a fight that was loosely connected to the truth: the less the homesteader knew, the less he was liable to pass on if Vickers came by.

"Maryjane's fixin' a meal just now," invited the farmer, "an' you're welcome to share."

Fisher shook his head, mumbling an excuse. He cleaned up at the water barrel on the porch, filled his canteen and paid two dollars for a small sack of grain and a hunk of cured meat. The farmer threw in a loaf of fresh bread for free. Fisher mounted up and rode on, carving strips of meat as he went.

He came on a wagon road heading west and

followed it. The going was faster here than through the breaks flanking the Missouri and he made good time. There were carts on the trail, mostly lumbering farm wagons drawn by dull-eyed oxen or deep-chested plough horses, but every so often a neat two-in-hand or a single rider showed. Towards nightfall he fell in alongside a flatbed carrying a homesteader and his wife towards some destination he never bothered to ask about. Northville, they told him, lay off to the south, about a day and a half distant. They invited him to ride with them and spend the night at their cabin, but Fisher refused, heading the black horse off in the direction the farmer indicated.

He rode until it got too dark to see and made camp, more concerned to rest the horse than with his own condition. That, he felt, was improving, his anger blocking out the pain as his bruises slowly mended. He reckoned to be a clear day ahead of Vickers by now: a lone rider could move faster than a mob, and he had wasted little time stopping to eat or sleep.

He knew that he needed rest; more important, that his mount needed to ease up for a while, so he made camp. He risked a small fire, heating coffee from his saddle bags as he chewed on the dried meat and the last of the bread. He fed the horse enough of the grain to replenish its strength without stuffing its belly so full it would be lethargic, then settled down to sleep.

The screeching of a jaybird woke him and he sat up, wiping dew from his face. The fire was dead, the small pile of dry twigs reduced to cold ash. He tugged his blanket about his shoulders, stumbling over to the horse. Doling out a few handfuls of grain, he watered the animal and threw the saddle on its back. His watch showed five in the morning.

Mist was rising from the land around him, a pale sun doing its best to filter through moisture. Fisher mounted up, wishing that he had a coat.

The country was flattening out now, the rolling hills giving way to the Kansas plains. Wheatfields shone bright in the sun, the waving yellow heads undulating in the wind, and well-worn trails became more frequent the farther he rode. He held the horse to a fast pace, halting three times during the day to rest the animal, alternating bursts of speed with an easier canter.

That night he slept rough again. Hungry, too, with his food gone.

In the morning he stopped long enough to swallow some hot biscuits and coffee, getting his bearings from the farmer who invited him to dismount and rest a spell.

The rest lasted just long enough for him to swallow one cup and cram three biscuits into his mouth. They were hard, and pained his jaw where the tooth had been smashed loose.

Some time before noon he sighted Northville.

The place was as McGarry had described it. With one exception. Fisher had anticipated a busy town, busier than usual if Brad was organising some kind of defence. But when he halted on the ridge to the north the place looked deserted, as though the citizens had left it, or were battening down in preparation for a Kansas twister.

He heeled the stallion to a fast canter, heading down the dusty trail that became main-street. Something had happened, something that felt wrong, and he loosened the Colt in its holster on his belt, letting his right hand hang loose by the stock of the Sharps carbine sheathed along his saddle.

As he entered the town a man stepped out from the shade of a porch. Sunlight flashed bright on his face, sparking off the gold frames of his spectacles. He carried a rifle cradled in his arms, a long-barrelled model, like the old woodsmen used.

Fisher whooped. It was Bradford McGarry.

He kicked the tired horse onwards, grinning as he saw McGarry's worry-creased face, the disapproving twist of his mouth.

"Brad!" he shouted, reining in. "How you doing?"

"Where the hell have you been?" was all McGarry said. Then, "Where's Vickers?"

"Behind me." Fisher climbed out of the saddle, sensing the wrongness of the place. "About a day behind. Things went wrong."

"You're damn' right they did." McGarry's voice was flat, toneless. "About as wrong as they could."

Fisher shrugged. "It don't exactly go to plan, but what the hell. We got a clear day to get ready. They'll ride into a trap the same as we figured."

"No," said McGarry, and his shoulders slumped. "No, they won't. There isn't any trap. There's only us."

"What?" Fisher spun round, staring down the empty street. "What about Wilde? The people here?"

"There's no one," said McGarry softly. "Just us. You and me."

"Oh damn," snarled Fisher.

And spat in the dust.

11

JONAS VICKERS pulled his men to a halt five miles clear of Northville. He thought that was far enough out to avoid detection, and he wanted some time to rest the horses and decide his next move.

They ate the last of the food they had brought with them as they rested, anxious to move on, but equally aware of the dangers of running blind into a possible ambush.

The men were tired: they had ridden hard since finding Jubal Farrow and Kyle Medlow dead in the old mill. The bodies had raised Vickers to heights of fury none of them had seen before, but the worst spur goading his rage was the escape of Lee Fisher.

The outlaw leader had been anticipating Fisher's execution. Had it all worked out in his mind. It was to be a formal affair, the Northern spy renounced as a traitor, an infiltrator, an agent of the yankee government that was trying to destroy the South and kill the spirit of a free society. Along with the profits of slavery and border raiding.

Then they would hang him.

Finding Kyle with his chest blown away and Jubal with half his face missing and a piece of rusty metal shoved into his belly, that had spoiled Vickers' neat plans.

He set his two best trackers, Jace and Vinny, to seeing where Fisher had gone. The tracks went west, so Vickers took his men that way. It was the right direction for Northville and the Southerner began to wonder if Fisher wasn't looking to reach his partner there and join in whatever plan they had set up.

He thought about it as he rode.

In the manner of a jigsaw the pieces began to fall into place. Fisher and the woman had been sent to Independence to work on the inside while someone else got Wilde ready for the planned attack. That could mean the yankees had a trap waiting, though it would be difficult to spring without word from Fisher. He wondered if killing Beaumont had been part of the plan, or an accident. The fat pig had been careless enough to risk his cover for the sake of a woman's body, so maybe his death was just bad luck. If so, the woman was shacked up in

Lawrence—a detail to be settled later—with Fisher running and Northville wondering what was coming.

Reports from his informers suggested that the military presence was fully occupied: he doubted that any troops would show when they hit the town.

That left Robert Wilde and his men along with the other agent. Vickers weighed the odds. Wilde's supporters were mostly cowboys and farmers; there were, maybe, six gunmen hired in. Seven with the agent. Not enough to stop his crew of thirteen hard-nosed Missouri Jayhawkers.

Fisher might be able to warn them, but he doubted it: the man was too badly hurt to ride far. The beating he got in the saloon must have weakened him enough that he was slower than the Captain's Band. There was small chance of a man going far, or fast, after that kind of foot-stomping.

But they hadn't found Fisher along the trail, even though two of the farms they had burned on the way talked of seeing a tall man in blood-stained clothes headed west. The description fitted and the idea that Fisher was staying ahead against all odds sat heavy and troublesome on Vickers' mind.

When they reached Northville the thin man called Caleb James over.

"Captain?" James was acting like the war had started and he was Vickers' second in command. It wasn't a bad idea at that. Caleb was no military thinker, but he knew how to follow orders, which was what Vickers wanted right now.

"Listen," he said, walking James away from the others. "There's no telling where that damn' spy's gone. He might have struck north. Maybe dropped off along the road. Then again, he could be down there."

He pointed towards the ridge hiding them from sight of the town.

"It ain't likely," grunted James, "not the way I broke him up."

"Godammit, Caleb!" Vickers' whisper was worse than a shout. "Will you shut your mouth and listen? He could be there. Probably not, but it's possible. And if he is, I want him. Me. No one else. You understand? If we sight him, you call the men off. Come with me, but leave him to me. All right?"

James nodded, wincing as Vickers' fingers bit

into his arm. "Sure, Captain. Whatever you say."

"Good. Now let's go."

They called for the outlaws to mount up and took them out. They rode two abreast until they reached the ridge, then halted as Vickers' raised his arm.

"Listen to me!" he shouted. "We're wiping this place off the damn' map! Understand? Anyone tries to stop us, we kill them. Anyone at all. If you see a man with a gun, you kill him. Women, too! We're striking a blow for the Southland that won't be forgotten. Remember that bastard Brown and Pottawatomie Creek. We'll pay that back and take Northville for the South. And that'll make us all rich."

A ragged cheer lifted through the still air.

"One thing," Vickers added. "The spy is mine. I'll shoot the man who touches him."

He walked his horse forwards, not waiting for an answer, easing the beast up to breast the ridge. Behind him the band spread out, forming into a rough skirmish line. Vickers led off at a trot, letting his horse make its own speed as he came down the ridge.

As they approached Northville, he urged the horse up gradually to a faster pace. Looping the

175

reins around his saddlehorn, he tugged matched Navy Colts from the holsters belted to either side of the saddle. Behind him, men drew rifles and handguns, some taking the reins in their teeth, others following Vickers' example.

The pace increased, building up to a canter. Then a run.

Then to a full gallop that swept them down at Northville in a rolling wave of yelling, wild-eyed hatred.

They went past the windmill that marked the eastern end of mainstreet. Guns thundered, shattering windows, spilling water from the barrels set to catch rain.

Then a man appeared before them.

He had both his arm raised wide to either side of his body, hands empty. He was dressed in a faded black jacket and newer pants. A grubby collar stood stiff and once-white around his neck.

"Peace!" he shouted, trying to make his voice heard over the hoofbeats. "Peace, my friends. Welcome to Northville."

Vickers reined in and the outlaws turned their horses in a circle about the man.

"I bid you welcome, brothers. Welcome in the name of the Lord. You need not come here

176

with guns in your hands, for we are peaceful folk. We intend you no harm. Nor is there need for you to harm us. Our town is yours. You are welcome . . ."

"Jesus Christ!" snarled Vickers. "It's a preacher come to greet us."

"A fuckin' preacher," echoed James.

And triggered the sawed-off shotgun.

Grubby white was abruptly red. The preacher toppled backwards, most of his face missing. He stretched his length in the dust and as the horsemen moved forwards his body was ground down into the road by the hooves that trampled him with casual indifference.

"Shit, this is gonna be easy," grinned Caleb James. "We even got welcomed."

A shot punctuated his sentence and off to his left a man cried out and fell from his horse. A second shot, louder than the first, echoed through the afternoon. A second outlaw tumbled, lifted clear of his saddle by the force of the bullet.

The raiders kicked their horses to a gallop, charging blind down the empty street. On either side windows and doors were drawn tight, heavy storm-shutters covering the openings. Their bullets blew jagged splinters from the woodwork, but no human targets showed. Vickers took them up to the far end of main-street and turned his horse. A dog, a ragged bundle of pale brown and dirty grey, ran out from the cattle pens, snapping irritably at the horses. A man cursed, fighting his mount to a stop. Beside him a gun barked and the little dog yelped once, snapping at the hole in its ribs. Its cries ended as the horses went over it.

Vickers took them back down the street.

Again the hidden rifle cracked, backed by the throatier roar of a heavy calibre carbine.

A horse went down coughing blood and a man lifted his arms wide as his face exploded and he somersaulted backwards over his saddle.

The horse stretched across the street, its rider climbing slowly to his feet, a Spencer carbine clutched in one hand, the other wiping dust from his eyes.

The hidden guns sounded again. The man jerked sideways, his right arm lifting up as a bullet broke his shoulder.

He stood for a moment before the second shot tore through his ribs and he crumpled like a fallen doll.

Vickers rode back down the street firing blind at walls and windows and rooftops. Halfway along he turned his horse off to the side, heading between two buildings for the outside of town. Caleb James took his lead and turned the other way. Four men followed him, five went with Vickers.

Only seven rode clear because the guns echoed again and two men, one to either side of the street, pitched from their horses with blood flecking their shirts and bullets ploughing death through their bodies.

The raiders went out and through, and for a while there was silence. Vickers headed back towards the windmill, taking his four men with him. They reined in, waiting for Caleb and the others to join them. When he took a count, Vickers was surprised at his losses. His original band was cut down to seven men.

It was hard to understand how, because he was sure that only two guns had contested their attack: scarce enough to down six men.

He set to grouping them again, readying for another charge.

But a shot interrupted his orders.

It rang loud; a dull, thundering sound that he had not heard in the melée of the attack.

A man stood suddenly upright in his stirrups, his right arm reaching over to clutch at the red hole in his left shoulder. He twisted sideways as another, softer, bark plucked a third eye from his forehead. He kept on twisting, slumping over and out of the saddle as his horse took fright and lit off to the north.

Down the street Lee Fisher looked over to the roof where Brad McGarry was thumbing a fresh load into the old Mississippi rifle, and motioned at the ground below. McGarry nodded his agreement, so Lee shifted back from the edge of William Canter's hardware store and jumped to the street.

So far they had done pretty well, he thought. Two against thirteen was long odds, even when the thirteen were facing expert marksmen with the advantage of height and lethal guns. He cradled the big Sharps .50 as he hit the dirt behind Canter's store. It was too good a gun to risk dropping, and he still needed it.

Though maybe not quite yet: the next part would most likely depend on pistol work.

He tucked the buffalo gun into the scabbard canted forwards along his saddle and patted the big black horse. Soon that speed might be needed.

He checked the load in the Navy Colt

holstered at his waist and walked down the alley between the Canter store and the Armelia Harris Millinery Emporium towards the street.

He wasn't sure that McGarry's plan would work, but it was all they had. And he wasn't about to let Brad walk out to face seven hard-case gunhands on his own. So he stepped out into the street, his jacket tucked back behind the butt of the Colt, grinning as he saw McGarry coming out to join him.

They met dead centre of mainstreet.

McGarry had his jacket hiked back to show the shoulder holster he favoured, though it was empty now, the Navy Colt in his hand. Fisher sided him, moving a few paces off to give his partner room.

There were seven men facing them, up at the far end of Northville's mainstreet, and no help likely to come. Fisher had his Colt loaded to the full six cylinders—assumed McGarry did too—which meant they carried twelve shots for seven men with two guns apiece. Horses, too.

Long odds.

Fisher hoped they weren't too long.

Hoped, too, that they were long enough to work McGarry's plan.

It was simple enough, worked out as they

waited for Vickers to come. Reason, pleas, even threats, had failed to rouse support amongst the citizens of Northville: if the raiders were to be resisted, it would be Fisher and McGarry on their own. They had agreed that sniping the attackers would whittle down the odds in the beginning, but it couldn't win the fight. Once the Jayhawkers had the two men spotted, it could be only a question of time before they were picked off or burned out. The logical answer was to run. Far and fast, leaving Northville to the mercy of Jonas Vickers. For different reasons neither McGarry or Fisher even considered the possibility.

Brad was determined to stay out of his obstinate sense of duty. Lee wanted to kill Vickers and James. So they formulated a plan accordingly.

After whittling the raiders down some, they would confront the men. If they could be provoked into attacking head-on, more would die and they might get mad enough to be careless. McGarry and Fisher would take off in different directions, hopefully dividing the attackers and leading them away from Northville.

After that . . .

Well, after that it would be down to luck and good shooting.

Fisher thumbed back the hammer of his Colt, heard the echo as McGarry followed suit. Then Vickers shouted an order and the horsemen were coming back down mainstreet.

The saddle of a galloping horse is no sound base for accurate shooting. A rifle, or carbine, is cumbersome, difficult to handle while riding; and a handgun becomes wildly inaccurate. A man on foot can sight and fire with far more confidence of hitting his target.

The two agents were basing their hopes— their lives—on that.

But even so, it was a scary proposition.

Gunsmoke preceded the riders like the froth of foam on the crest of a wave. The staccato bark of detonating cartridges rang loud in the warm air. The two men held their ground, waiting for the outlaws to come within range.

Then Fisher triggered a shot and broke to the side of the street. He ducked behind the cover of a rain barrel, firing as the raiders went by him. Dust and smoke clouded his vision, acrid with the smell of sweat and gunpowder. He rolled off the porch as the horses thundered on to the far end of Northville, glancing back to count three bodies sprawled in the dust.

Climbing on to the black horse, he made a fast mental calculation. Vickers. James. Two others. The odds grew better, coming down in his favour.

He slammed his heels into the animal's ribs, raising a miniature duststorm as he headed out of town. On the other side of Northville, McGarry did the same.

At the far end of mainstreet Vickers grouped his men, pale eyes wild as he counted his losses. Caleb; Jace McAllister; Tobe Hooper; himself. Hell! Was that all? Had Fisher and his goddamned partner wiped out the whole bunch? He looked up as a shout from the street caught his attention. Someone stood up, right arm hanging limp, a Colt Dragoon still clutched in the left hand. Vickers recognised the man: Mort Carson. And he was waving them towards him.

Carson was hit in the arm. Blood was pulsing over his shirt sleeve, but he was too angry to notice the pain. He pointed with his revolver as Vickers and the others reached him.

"They went off in diff'rent directions. Had horses up the side o' the buildings."

"Fisher! Where'd he go?" Vickers' dry voice snarled. "Tall man in a dark suit. You see him?"

"Yeah." Carson nodded, pointing south. "He lit off that way. Ridin' a black horse."

Vickers didn't answer, just pulled his horse round, shouting for Caleb James to follow him.

"Jace, Tobe. You go after the other one."

The four men separated, spurring their horses in pursuit.

Mort Carson was left dumbstruck and bleeding in the middle of mainstreet. He shouted after them, but his cry was lost in the pounding of the hooves and he cursed, looking down the street to where his own mount was pawing dust beside the cattle pens. He began to walk.

Over to his left a shutter banged open. Carson turned, levelling his gun on the window. A woman's face ducked back out of sight. He spun as a second shutter thudded wide. A man stared at him, as though daring him to fire.

The doors of the hotel opened and a man stepped out. He was unarmed, just stood, watching Carson pace nervously towards his horse. More shutters swung out from darkened windows, faces studying the outlaw as he walked down the street. Ahead and to his right a woman stepped into view. She was dressed in a faded calico print, grey hair tugged back into a heavy knot at the nape of her neck. Her face was pale, scoured dry by sun and wind, her eyes huge, red with weeping.

She let the door swing shut behind her, crossing the boardwalk with an even tread that might have been measured or just slow. Carson stared at her as she eased herself down on to the street and moved out to face him.

Nervously, he aimed his pistol at her breasts.

"He was one of them!" Her voice was harsh as her face, almost devoid of tone. "He helped to kill my husband."

Carson heard more doors open, glanced around. People were coming into view now, coming out on to porches and boardwalks. Watching. Watching *him*.

"Get the hell back!" He waved his gun. "I'll kill the man as tries to stop me!"

"And the woman?"

She was walking towards him, one arm lifted to point. Carson felt his mouth go suddenly dry.

"You killed my husband. Shot him down and rode him into the ground. He was a good man. Better than you. You shouldn't have killed him." She spoke as she walked, still aiming that accusing finger at his face. "An eye for an eye, that's what the Book says. A tooth for a tooth. Your life for his."

"Crazy goddam bitch!" Carson levelled the Dragoon at her face. "You get the hell outta my path, or I'll kill you."

She stopped a foot from him, her arm dropping to her side. Carson gulped, halting himself as her pale, tear-glistened eyes stared at his dirty face. He heard movement behind him, around him, and turned to see what was happening.

The street was filling up. Men with pistols and rifles were moving into view. Some held shotguns, one or two carried axes or pick hafts. There were women, too. Holding knives and cooking skewers, some barehanded.

All converged on the centre of the street.

Carson rammed his gun into the woman's stomach.

"You try anything an' she's dead!" He wished he could use his right arm, tug the woman against him to act as a shield. "I'm tellin' you, she's dead!"

The crowd slowed, circling around him.

Waiting.

The woman halted. She looked at Carson, then away up the street to where the broken body of the preacher lay bloody in the dust.

"You killed my husband," she said. Quiet and flat. "An eye for an eye. A life for a life."

She reached out, grabbing the Colt. Her hands closed around the cylinder, locking tight as she yanked the pistol hard against her belly. The sudden movement tore apart the final remnants of Carson's nerves. He squeezed the trigger, and was almost as startled as the crowd when the woman flew backwards, a great red stain erupting over the front of her dress.

He thumbed the hammer, panic taking hold, and ran forwards.

A man loomed before him, aiming a rusty-barrelled Colt. Carson shot him, pushing the body aside before it had time to fall. He fired once more before his gun was empty. Saw a woman with a cleaver raised high over her head stumble back with blood spilling from her stomach and mouth.

Then he was running for his horse, the Dragoon dropped and forgotten in the bloody dust of Northville.

He almost reached the pony before the first bullet hit him. It went in beneath his right shoulder, spinning him round so that he faced back towards the crowd. The second twisted him again. It tore through his right hip, turning him back in a half circle as a third shot blew his left leg from under him.

He collapsed into the dust. The bullets seemed unreal: there was no pain, only a great fear as he saw the crowd close in.

A woman lifted a greasy knife. Plunged the blade down. Carson screamed as he felt the point tear deep into his stomach.

Then there was only pain. The crowd cutting, shooting, clubbing.

Northville took its revenge, now that the odds were safe.

12

McGARRY rode north, making for the ridge. If he could reach that in time, he would have the advantage of height and the narrowed trail to pick off the two men following him.

If he could reach it.

They were closer than he liked, but riding carelessly, bunched together in their eagerness to take him. He halted his pony and tugged the Mississippi rifle clear of the scabbard. He turned his horse sideways on to the trail and brought the rifle to his shoulder.

Fired.

And saw one man go down.

He fumbled powder into the barrel, tamped it. Dropped a heavy lead ball into the hungry muzzle and wadded a twist of cloth tight over the charge.

A percussion cap on the nipple of the firing pan. Sight. Cock. Fire . . .

The man rising to his feet beside the body of his dead horse threw up his arms and fell back.

McGarry swung his own mount round, urging it up to a gallop as he sought to gain distance on the man still moving after him.

A rifle barked and he felt something whistle past his face. Twisted in the saddle to peer back.

Jace McAllister was still coming at him, cursing as he dragged a Colt from his belt and checked the load. Three shots left. Enough to handle this goddam yankee. He checked the distance between them. Ten minutes, maybe fifteen, before he was close enough to use the pistol effectively. He lifted his horse to a gallop, intent on closing up the distance.

McGarry slid the rifle back into the saddle bucket and rode away. His own handgun was empty, and before he could risk slowing enough to reload he needed some space between them.

He set to making it.

Jace's horse was winded, McGarry's fresh. The man in the drab brown suit spaced out the distance. Jace cursed, urging his pony to a last, desperate effort. He was conscious of the need to catch the yankee before the man got time to reload. Catch him and kill him.

If it went that way.

McGarry recognised the alternatives and

concentrated on building distance. After a while, he looked back and decided he could risk an attempt at reloading. He wound his reins about the saddlehorn and steered the horse with his knees as he hauled the Navy Colt clear of the shoulder holster. Reaching into his jacket pocket he tugged a handful of ready-made cartridges free. He dropped the first one, but the second and third slid snug into the chambers of the Navy Colt. He fumbled one more into the gun and decided that was enough. The lead balls followed, tamped down into the waxed paper of the cartridges with the ramrod hinged under the barrel.

Then the really hard part: capping the cylinders at full gallop.

McGarry swore uncharacteristically as the first and second percussion caps fell loose. The man behind was closing up fast enough to get a shot in before the gun was ready to fire. Still swearing, he risked capping the shots fast, tamping when all three chambers were full-loaded. It might easily have resulted in accidental back-flash, detonating the gun while it was still in his hand. But that was a better chance than risking a bullet in the back.

He grunted as the last cylinder was rammed

tight and ready to use, glancing back to check the distance.

The rider was almost within range, urging his foam-flecked horse to a last desperate effort. McGarry saw a cut show ahead of his path, a low-walled ravine leading off to the west. He turned his horse into the gulley.

Behind him Jace McAllister followed, anticipating the kill.

McGarry rode headlong down the cut, waiting.

Then it showed: a spill of hard-packed sand leading up to the rim. He turned his horse, urging the beast up the slope. At the top he reined in, waiting for Jace to show.

The outlaw came on at full gallop. McGarry saw his face clearly, eyes slitted against the rising dust and mouth set in a thin line as he concentrated on the pursuit. He went past and McGarry came down off the rim, moving fast to come up behind Jace. The man didn't hear him over the sound of his hoof beats.

Not until McGarry was up close enough to touch him with the Navy Colt.

The outlaw tensed in surprise, turning his head to look back. He twisted, trying to bring his own gun into play, but before he could line the barrel, McGarry fired.

The shot lifted Jace up and forwards, tipping him over the horse's neck. The animal stumbled and McGarry fired again as he went past. Jace was blown sideways, blood exploding from his ribs and spine. He fell from the saddle, his weight dragging the horse over so that it shied and tried to kick the body away.

McGarry hauled his own mount to a stop, turning it to walk back to the body stretched in the dust of the gulley.

Jace's horse snickered anxiously as he came alongside, and McGarry reached out to pat the animal, calming it. He dismounted and looked down at the fallen outlaw. Jace was spread-eagled on the ground, the front of his shirt bloody where McGarry's bullet had emerged through his stomach. Under his back a spreading pool of red was cloying the sand. McGarry kicked the body hard, checking. There was no movement, only a few angry flies buzzing up from the unexpected feast.

McGarry loaded his pistol, then hauled the rifle clear of the saddle and reloaded that. When he was finished, he looked up at the sky, breathing a long sigh of relief.

Afternoon was shading into evening, and where the walls of the gulley blocked off the sun it was cold.

Cold as a grave on a warm summer day.

McGarry climbed back on his horse and rode away in the direction of Northville.

Jace's horse watched him go, then whinnied softly and shook its head, tugging the reins free of the dead hand. It began to trot after McGarry. Brad heard it coming and paused. He waited until the animal caught up with him, then reached over to lift the trailing reins. The outlaw wouldn't be needing a mount again and the horse might turn a useful profit.

He wondered how Lee was doing.

Fisher was looking for a place to make a stand. The black horse was beginning to tire, its strength tested by the fast ride from Independence. Vickers and James were riding fresher animals, and closing the gap.

The country south of the town offered no useful gulleys or ridges from which to mount an ambush, running flat and empty towards the Arkansas river. The two men were close enough that one would reach him even if he dropped the other, ride him down as he reloaded. He gritted his teeth and concentrated on urging the stallion to hold its pace.

He was surprised that Vickers should press the chase so far, Northville was out of sight now and the deeper the outlaws rode into Kansas, the greater became the chance of someone organising a legal posse to go after them. He guessed that Vickers had stopped thinking about that, had given himself up to his desire for revenge. Fisher grinned at the thought: it suited his purpose. The memory of Knowles and Marsh was still bitter in his mind, two killings he owed the raiders.

If he could work it right.

He moved on, one part of his mind fixed on the chase, the other working out how he would kill them.

Not the Sharps, he decided. Not if he could avoid it. The big carbine was capable of dropping them both at a half-mile or more, but that was too impersonal. That part of his mind fashioned in its thinking by the Blackfeet who had raised him demanded personal vengeance, to see their faces as his bullets hit them. Savagely, with the cold fury of the Indian warriors, he wanted them to know it was him, no-one else, who pulled the trigger, who had destroyed their dreams of power and of money.

If he could stay alive that long.

He glanced off to his right, narrowing his eyes against the glare of the setting sun. It would be dark soon, and in the night he could circle round . . .

He looked back. Half a mile, maybe a little more. Enough, anyway, to hold the distance until the sun went down.

The black was blowing hard as twilight fell and he knew the horse must rest soon or die. He went through a stand of hickory and cedar, the thick foliage hiding him as he emerged on to a wide meadow that sloped down to a creek. To his right, the land lifted slightly in a kind of hummock, almost invisible in the growing darkness. He turned in that direction, jumping from the saddle as he reached the far side of the hump. Hauling down on the reins, he yanked the horse's left foreleg upwards, wrestling the startled beast over on its side. He threw himself across its neck, one hand clamped tight around its muzzle.

He waited. And was rewarded by the sound of hoofbeats, the sight of two shadowy figures emerging from the trees.

They reined in, scanning the slope, and Fisher heard them calling to one another as they checked the ground.

"Jesus!" He recognised Caleb James' voice. "I can't see a damn' thing. He could be anywhere."

"Keep looking." That was Vickers. "He can't be far ahead."

"Yeah; but where? I ain't no goddam injun that I can see a trail in the dark."

"He's running. Most likely he went straight on ahead. We'll try that direction."

"An' if we don't find him? What then?"

"Hell!" Vickers sounded bitter. "We'll turn off east, make our way to Independence."

Their shouts faded away towards the creek and Fisher relaxed a little. He waited a few minutes, listening. There was the splash of hooves churning water, then the distant sound of the two men going up the far slope. He stood up, letting the black horse climb to its feet. It stood, head down and panting, while Fisher reloaded the carbine and handgun. When he was finished he walked the animal down to the creek and let it drink, splashing water over his face and hands as he thought about his next move.

Vickers and James wouldn't ride too far in the dark, not with the likelihood of an ambush somewhere ahead. No, they'd make camp and try to pick up his trail come morning. Only then the situation would be reversed. It would be him hunting them.

The thought warmed his empty belly as he settled down to sleep.

When the sun came up, their tracks showed clear in the dew-wetted grass. Fisher followed the marks at an easy canter, resting his horse. They went down to the stream, then up the far side of the slope. He slid the buffalo gun from the saddle boot as he approached the ridge. No shot came so he walked the horse almost to the crest, then dismounted and crawled to the top. The grass ran on in an unbroken vista towards a line of low hills. There were thickets of wild mulberry and occasional trees dotting the plain, and he saw that the tracks led directly to one such windbreak.

The ashes of a small fire showed beyond the bushes and when he sifted the grey dust through his fingers it was still warm. The sun was up now, drying out the grass so that the hoof prints became indistinct, but he saw that they went on towards the south, heading for the hills.

He mounted and rode in that direction.

He used all his Indian training to make out the trail. Here there was a patch of crushed grass where one of the men had halted, turning his horse to check behind. There a pile of droppings. Snagged on the spikes of a thorn bush he found a fragment of torn cloth; farther on, a paper cartridge, dropped and discarded. The signs were invisible to the inexperienced eye, and even Fisher had trouble spotting them. It took time, but it told him what he needed to know: they were swinging gradually to the east, making for the Missouri border.

Around mid-morning he saw smoke drifting lazily from below the hills, a little later there was the distant outline of buildings. He rode towards them.

It was a settlement, built in close to the edge of the rock. A road went up through a low pass and Fisher wondered if the two men had gone that way or stopped in the town.

There was only one way to find out.

He paused beside a wind-weathered signpost. Someone had used a hot iron to score a name into the bleached wood: Skylar. Underneath was a figure, scored out to be replaced by another that looked like 32. Fisher grinned: it shouldn't be hard to find two strangers here.

Flipping the safety thong clear of the Colt's hammer, he went into Skylar.

From the holes cut into the rockface above the town, and the tumbled frames of winding gear and wash-trenches, he guessed that the place had once been a mining community. That looked to be in the long ago, the mines now worked-out and the town run down with them. There was a livery stable that looked as though few people used it, and a few huts; two stores with fly-speckled windows and not much on display; a low, shed-like building with a faded sign boasting of food and beds; and a saloon.

Fisher ignored the curious stares of the handful of people moving along the street as he reined in outside the saloon. There were two small windows cut into the timber on either side of a narrow door, both smoked over and cracked. A neat, round hole radiated a web pattern low down in one window, about the height of a man's stomach.

Fisher pushed his coat back and rested his right hand on the butt of the Colt as he went in.

He moved quickly to one side of the door, his eyes probing the gloom. It was a low-ceilinged, lonely-looking room, bare timber running out from the natural rock forming the rear wall. There were no other doors and only three people in the place. Fisher walked to the bar and turned to face the door.

The bar was two planks set on a line of barrels, dark watermarks and the remains of dead flies emphasising the hopelessness of the miserable place. The glass the bartender pushed over looked almost as dirty.

"Whisky?"

Fisher nodded. "And beer."

"Sure."

The whisky was almost colourless, a fierce, home-brewed concoction that burned his throat as it went down. The beer was flat and warm. The bartender looked torn between defiance and apology, as though expecting a comment on the quality of his goods.

Instead, Fisher tapped the glass, studying the other occupants as the whisky splashed over the brim. Two were old men dressed in patched and faded shirts that had been washed often enough to bleach out whatever colour they had started with. After glancing once in his direction, they went back to their cards, ignoring him. The third was a woman, her looks faded as the ancient shirts. Her hair was reddish, grey streaks showing through where the henna had failed to reach. She wore a tacky scarlet dress, stained dark beneath the arms, and a slack smile on her garish lips.

Her eyes were tired, dead-looking, as she raised plucked brows in unspoken question.

Like the bartender, she looked as though she expected a refusal.

"No thanks." Fisher forestalled her question. "I don't have the time."

"The story of my life." She said it without rancour, accustomed to rejection. "'Lady, I don't have the time'. That's if they remember to add the 'lady'."

She sat down again, absently twirling a strand of loose hair around a nail-bitten finger, staring out through the door at nothing.

Fisher turned to the barman. "I'm looking for two men. You seen any strangers?"

The man shrugged, wiping idly at a dirty glass.

Fisher dropped a coin beside the whisky bottle. The bartender stared at it without making a move. Fisher threw a second coin down. It jangled as it spun against his glass.

"That help your memory any?"

The man shrugged. "Might do. What they look like?"

"Hell!" Fisher drained his beer. "How many strangers d'you get through here?"

"Enough. I don't pay too much notice. It ain't my job."

"One's thin and dressed in black," said Fisher patiently. "Pale face and blue eyes, kind of scarey. The other's a big man with a black beard. Wears two pistols."

"Well," the bartender nodded slowly, "I guess I mighta noticed two fellers answerin' to that description. I'd hafta think about it, though."

He stared at the coins, then up at Fisher. Waiting.

Fisher reached down as though looking for another coin. Instead, his hand came up with the Colt's Navy pointed at the man. He set the gun down next to the coins and casually eased the hammer back. The *click* sounded loud.

"Don't take too long," he said quietly.

The bartender went pale under his stubble and gulped.

"This mornin'. They rode in askin' questions same as you. Said somethin' about gettin' fresh horses an' a meal. They might be up at Cargill's stable or down to Vern Johnson's eatery. I don't know."

Fisher eased the hammer down and holstered the pistol. "Thanks."

He finished the whisky and turned away. As he reached the door the bartender's voice stopped him.

"Hey mister, you forgot to pay fer the drinks."

"Go to hell," said Fisher without looking back.

He stepped out on to the sidewalk and glanced along the street. There were a couple of cowboys playing mumbley peg outside one of the stores and a cluster of old men dozing in the sun. The only horses in sight belonged to the cowboys, apart from Fisher's own animal, so he walked towards the eating house.

Outside, he drew his gun and cocked it. Then he slammed his foot hard against the door, going through as the wood sprang back to clatter against the wall. Seven people looked up as he went in and a woman screamed, dropping a pile of dirty plates. Fisher ignored the noise, pointing the Colt down the room at Caleb James.

The big man was coming to his feet with food spilling from his mouth and the shotgun in his right hand.

"Don't!" Fisher snarled.

James let the scattergun fall to the floor.

"Where's Vickers?"

Two women and a man sidled nervously past him, running as they got to the door. Fisher ignored them, his eyes fixed on James. A man in a grubby apron stuck his head out from the kitchen, then ducked back inside as he realised what was happening. Four more men backed warily away from the single table.

"You'll find out," grunted James. "When he puts a bullet in yore back."

Fisher moved so that the wall was behind him, the open door on his right. "Where is he?"

"Go to hell," rasped the bearded man. "What you gonna do? Gun me down here? In front o' witnesses?"

"No," said Fisher, his voice cold. "Not here. Out on the street."

He motioned for the onlookers to move back from the table and walk around behind Caleb. They hurried to obey. Then he stepped carefully sideways, shifting back from the door so that James would have no chance to touch him as he went by.

Outside, he pointed to the centre of the single, dusty track. "Down there. I'll give you a better chance than Knowles or Marsh got."

Caleb James sneered and stepped down. Fisher glanced up the street: there was no sign of Vickers. He followed James and paced off twelve steps, aware of people coming out like vultures with the scent of dying meat in the air. Still watching the big man, he lowered the hammer of the Colt and dropped the pistol into the holster.

"Call it," he said.

Caleb James dropped to a crouch, his body turning sideways on to present a smaller target. His right hand went down to the gun on his right hip, snatching the big Dragoon up and out.

He was fast.

Almost as fast as Lee Fisher.

But not fast enough . . .

The Navy Colt roared once and James staggered back with blood staining the front of his shirt. His own gun blasted dust a yard clear of

Fisher's boots. Then he stumbled and went down. Fisher stood, waiting. The big man groaned, spitting blood over his beard. He pushed himself up, tugging at the second gun. When he turned to face Lee again he had both Dragoons in his hands.

Fisher let go a second shot. He had his arm stretched out, sighting on Caleb's face. The bullet hit the outlaw in the mouth, smashing his head back so that his guns fired wild, above Fisher's head. He twisted to the side, crumpling, blood spilled thick from his mouth and neck and Fisher smiled. There was no humour in it, only satisfaction.

He began to walk down the street in the direction of the livery stable, the Navy Colt held by his side.

Suddenly a horse exploded into view. It was hitting full stride as Fisher recognised the black-suited man crouched in the saddle. Vickers was firing two handed, blasting shots blind as he raced straight at Lee.

Fisher snapped off a shot, throwing himself to the side as Vickers tried to run him down. He couldn't see if it hit or missed and then the shoulder of the horse smashed into him, hurling him aside. He fell, winded, and rolled as a bullet creased his cheek.

Then Vickers was gone, riding hell-for-leather up the trail towards the pass.

13

THERE was dust in his mouth and the salt taste of blood. His chest hurt where the horse had crashed into him, and his ribs were aching again. He climbed to his feet, staring after Vickers.

The outlaw was a good way up the trail, almost at the pass where the high rocks would cover him. Fisher cursed and ran down the street, jamming his pistol back into the holster.

He reached his horse and looked back.

Damn! Vickers was too far gone to chase. With that kind of start he would be well into the rocks before Fisher got anywhere near him. Into the rocks and laying an ambush . . .

Riding up there under Vickers' gunsights would be pure madness.

Fisher hauled the Sharps clear of the saddle boot, checking the load as he ran back to the far side of mainstreet. From there the trail ran unobscured up into the rocks. There was a curve where it swung around an outcrop, but after that it headed arrow straight through the pass.

Fisher sat down in the dust, crossing his legs so that his knees stuck up in front of him. He licked his thumb and wiped a tiny bead of spittle on to the foresight. Vickers disappeared behind the outcrop. Fisher cocked the hammer. There was no time to elevate the adjustable rearsight: it was one shot or nothing. He took a deep breath, lining the droplet of spittle dead centre of the vee notch.

Vickers showed beyond the rock.

Fisher rested his elbows on his knees, calculating the distance . . .

A half mile? No: closer to three quarters. One hell of a long shot. But not too far.

He let his breath out gently. And squeezed the trigger.

The buffalo gun roared like a small cannon, slamming back against his shoulder hard enough to send a stab of pain through his ribs. The sound echoed around the cliffs. Fisher climbed to his feet.

From up the trail, faint in the distance, there was a high-pitched scream. Vickers' horse stumbled. Its head went down and its hindquarters lifted into the air. The animal somersaulted, legs flailing as the rider was catapulted from the saddle, crashing down yards ahead of the fallen beast.

Fisher stood, watching. Vickers climbed to his feet and ran back. For a moment he tugged on the reins, trying to drag the horse up. It was wasted effort. The horse was down for good. Fisher crossed to his own mount and slid the carbine into the scabbard. He hauled himself into the saddle and drove his heels into the animal's ribs.

The black horse took off at a gallop, scattering the onlookers as Fisher steered it fast out of Skylar. He headed straight towards the pass, watching Vickers as he rode.

The outlaw was dragging something from under his horse. Fisher recognised it as a rifle: he hoped it wasn't another buffalo gun. If it was, Vickers had no intention of using it yet. Instead, he turned and began to clamber over the rocks, moving towards the old mine workings. Fisher rode on, tensed to duck if Vickers should fire. He went past the outcrop and reined in alongside the wounded horse.

Jumping from the saddle, he lead his own mount to the near side of the trail, tethering it under cover of a jutting overhang. He pulled the Sharps from the boot and reloaded, then set the big carbine down as he primed the Navy Colt. Vickers' horse was snickering quietly, blood frothing from its nostrils. Fisher saw that his bullet had gone in just ahead of the animal's haunches, ploughing forwards through its stomach to shatter its right shoulder. He felt a momentary pang of sadness; then levelled the Colt on the beast's head and shot it neatly through the skull.

Holstering the pistol, he swung round, moving downtrail to where a spill of rock afforded a path up.

He found cover behind a boulder as he scanned the upper slopes. Above him and to his right, the hills flattened out, dropping in a smooth slope to the edge of the cliff overlooking Skylar. The downface was riddled with tunnels and rotting machinery; the intervening terrain jumbled with fallen rock and narrow ravines. Farther up there was a roadway that looked to be cut through the rock. It went off from the trail just below the pass, leading towards the old mines. Vickers was running along it, making for the disused shafts.

Fisher sighted the Sharps, trailing the outlaw like a hunter follows a pigeon's flight over open sights. It was an easy shot. One squeeze and Vickers would go down with a .50 calibre ball spreading his life over the lonely rocks.

Fisher lifted his finger clear of the trigger. It was too easy: Vickers deserved worse than that.

He moved out from the boulder, clambering over the rough ground after the outlaw.

Vickers was running now. Running scared. His plans of conquest and revenge were forgotten in the desperate need to stay alive. He seemed close to panic, heading blind for the refuge of the mine workings like some animal bolting for cover in the nearest dark hole.

Fisher began to smile as he went after the man. Maybe this way Vickers was learning what it felt like to have someone hunting you; maybe he was beginning to feel the fear his victims had known. Fisher hoped it was so: it satisfied his sense of personal vengeance.

He tried to keep sight of the running man as he worked his way up and across, moving to cut Vickers' path. It was difficult because the ground was broken up too much, the cuts he had to cross dropping him down out of sight, boulders and rock falls hiding Vickers. When he got to the open space leading on to the mines the outlaw was gone.

He paused, studying the terrain ahead. There was the flat area, rutted with wagon tracks as though it had once been used as a loading point, its downslope terminating in broken ground, ravines and rock spills. Above, the wall of a cliff rose sheer for several hundred feet. At the far side a flank of rock jutted out to narrow the rough trail, its lower end fallen away in a long drop down towards Skylar. The mine workings lay ahead, past that narrowing of the trail. Vickers, he guessed, had gone that way. Which meant that he had to go through the bottleneck.

He took it at a run, darting from boulder to boulder, hugging cover like a rabbit with a hawk in the sky. He reached the overspill and flattened back against the rock. Down below, Skylar was still bathed in sunlight; up on the high slopes shadows were stretching long and black over the rocks. The upper slopes, shaded by the crest of the hills, were dark now, making his pursuit even more dangerous. The rock face holding the mine openings would be in shadow, when he came out from behind the boulders he would be in sunlight: an easy target.

He thought about it for a moment, then looked up and began to climb over the bottleneck.

When he reached the top he thought he saw the glint of sun off metal, but it might have been some piece of forgotten machinery. It was a useless doubt, anyway: if he let darkness fall before he killed Vickers, the raider could get away in the night.

It had to be prior to sunset.

He came off the rocks in a wild, stumbling run that dropped him down on to the miniature plateau fronting the old mines.

Something moved and he threw himself to the right as a gun echoed across the stone.

Metal shrieked loud on rock close to his head. As he rolled behind the cover of a pulley tripod, he saw a long scorch mark on the stone, no more than one inch above his position. He bellied down behind the mouldering timbers of the pulley. It was scant cover, but the best he had until he could spot Vickers' position.

The outlaw gave it away with his second shot.

There was a flash, followed close by a spray of rotten wood that dropped maggoty timbers over Fisher's shoulders. He fired back, snapping off a shot at the second mine opening, listening to the ricochet as the heavy ball reverberated down the shaft.

"What the hell are you using?"

Vickers still sounded confident.

"A Sharps," yelled Fisher. "Buffalo gun. I can blast you out of there in pieces."

"The hell you can! You got to sight me first."

Fisher smiled. "Or starve you. You're not going nowhere."

"Maybe," called Vickers. "Maybe not. I reckon I can hold out long enough to kill you."

"Too long," shouted Fisher, reloading as he spoke. "You don't have a chance. Your horse is dead and I'm out here. Give up now. Throw your guns out and I'll give you a chance."

"The devil you will!" Vickers blew more wood from the pulley frame. "Who are you anyway?"

"The man who's gonna kill you," yelled Fisher. "I was hired to stop your raids. Guess I've done that, now."

"Don't lay bets! It's just you and me up here. And I'll lay odds I can take you."

"Go ahead and try." Fisher triggered another shot into the mine. "I owe you."

"Yeah," shouted Vickers, "I guess you do. How'd it feel, killing those citizens you were hired to protect?"

That hurt. It brought back too many sick memories. For an instant Fisher recalled

Knowles' toppling back into the flames of his ranch house, Jethro Marsh dancing on the end of the rope. There was a sour taste in his mouth as he shouted back his answer.

"It felt bad! That's why I want to kill you slow. Because of that!"

Vickers laughed. It was an eerie sound in the gathering dusk, as though he enjoyed laying a burden of guilt on Fisher even though the agent might kill him, as though it gave him some kind of warped satisfaction even though he might die as a result.

"Then you'd best come in and get me."

"Yeah," grunted Fisher.

And lifted up from behind the pulley, firing the Sharps as he ran across the open ground.

Vickers' bullet passed close over his left shoulder, and he spread his length in the dirt, rolling behind a rusty handcart. He counted the time it took for the second shot to come: maybe seven seconds. Hardly enough to cross the distance. Whatever kind of rifle the outlaw was using, it had to be a breechloader with ready-made cartridges, faster to prime than his own Sharps.

So: he had to get up close to the mine and flush Vickers out where the Colt would kill him.

And that before the sun went down. Which didn't leave him very long.

Regretting the mess it would make of his jacket, Fisher stretched out on his back, bracing both feet against the car.

He began to push as Vickers shouted again.

"What you waiting for yankee? I thought you were coming in to get me."

The car groaned, rust protesting the unaccustomed movement. Slowly, it began to shift, wheels grinding in shrill complaint. Fisher clasped both his hands over the old rails and ignored the agony filling his bruised body as he fought the thing loose from its position.

Splinters of rust lanced his hands and his legs felt as though they might break, but the car shifted, moving up-slope. He twisted over, coming up to set his left shoulder against the bulk of the wagon.

He manhandled it up towards the mine entrance, holding his head down as Vickers' bullets ricocheted loud off the metal. The bulk of the thing meant that he had to drop the Sharps, so he left the buffalo gun alongside the tracks and drew the Colt.

Vickers fired again.

The shot spanged off the bulk of the car.

A second time . . .

A third . . .

He was close to the mine.

A fourth bullet tumbled rust over his face.

Shadow pooled about him and he knew that he was there. Close enough to the shaft to block Vickers' escape. He glanced over his shoulder, studying the sky. The sun was going down now, the shadows lengthening over the upper slopes. The rockface was solid darkness, a black that stretched out towards the rim of the plateau as daylight faded away into the brief dusk that preceded full night.

A fifth shot echoed off the metal of the car, close enough to the mine shaft now that he felt the thud of the bullet ring through the wagon.

Then light flashed bright and noisy to his left.

A dark shadow ran out from the mine, flame bursting from one outstretched hand.

Fisher ducked, flattening back against the mine car. Two bullets thudded dull against the side, the last rattled off the near end, sharding metallic dust into his eyes.

He swung round to put the body of the car between him and Vickers, wiping urgently at his face.

Tears ran down his cheeks and he blinked

desperately, trying to clear his hurt eyes. Another shot ricocheted over his head and he dropped to a crouch, trying to see.

Moving blind, he stumbled to the front of the car, firing round it into the watery darkness. His shot was answered by the reverberation of the outlaw's gun. Then the thud of boots over the rock.

He fumbled the dust from his eyes and looked round the ore car.

Off towards the bottleneck he saw a dim figure running fast through the shadows. He came up to his full height, stretching both arms out over the edge of the car's wall. He clasped his left hand over his right, holding the Navy Colt rock steady, bracing against the kick.

He thumbed the hammer back. Sighted. Fired.

The shadow stumbled, tottered on. Fell.

Fisher came out from behind the car and walked towards the bottleneck.

Vickers was rolling over on to his back, hands fumbling at pockets and gun, shoving cartridges into the pistol.

"Stay back!" his voice rang loud off the dark rock. "Stay back or you're dead."

Fisher kept walking. Slowly now, savouring

the moment, letting his hate control him. He held the Navy Colt down by his side, watching Vickers reload.

"How's it feel," Loathing sounded thick in his voice. "You think the others felt like this? The ones you killed? Knowles and Marsh? You think they got scared when they knew they were going to die? How does it feel, Jonas Vickers?"

"I'm not gonna die!" Vickers sounded hysterical. "I can't! The South lives! You yankee bastards are the ones gonna die!"

He fired at Fisher.

The bullet flew wild and Fisher laughed.

"How many shots left, Vickers? Five?" He kept walking.

Vickers scuttered backwards, crabbing on elbows and heels. He fired again as he moved. And again the bullet blew loose of its target.

"Four?" called Fisher, dodging behind a rock.

Chips blew from the stone and he wondered if the outlaw had loaded on five cylinders, or the full six.

"God damn you to hell! Yankee bastard!" Vickers' voice was pitched up high now, strained with fear. "I had a good thing going."

"And I spoiled it." Fisher enjoyed the taunting. "And now I'm going to kill you."

"Not yet!" Vickers blasted another shot off the rock. "I'm not finished yet."

"You are!" Fisher darted to the side, fetching up behind a toppled crane. "You're a walking dead man, Vickers."

"No!" Vickers stood up, blasting wild into the darkness. "I'm Jonas Vickers! I can't die."

"You can," called Fisher. "I'm about to prove it."

He fired again, deliberately angling his shot down and to the left. He chuckled as Vickers jumped back, leaping clear of the dust that jumped about his feet.

"No!" Vickers ran back. "No!"

The light was almost completely gone, filling the ridge with darkness, except for the few places where the western rock was split wide enough to allow the last dying shafts through. Vickers ran towards one such cleft. It was a faster way down to the pass; to Fisher's horse. It was also one of the few places that spilled light through the shadows.

Fisher came out from behind the tumbled machinery and braced himself, legs spread wide as he held the Navy Colt out at arm's length.

"You're right," he murmured. "The answer is no."

Vickers was climbing over the rocks, clambering up towards the gap. Towards the safety of the trail. The escape offered by Fisher's horse. He moved fast, his gun almost forgotten now in his desperation.

He reached the topmost boulder and paused, glancing back.

Fisher watched, lining the Colt.

Red as blood, the sun outlined Jonas Vickers with an impersonal halo of light.

Fisher squeezed the trigger.

The outlaw fell back, arms flying up as he lost his footing and crashed down on the far side of the gap. Fisher broke into a run, heading straight for the split.

He went over the rocks fast, anxious that Vickers should not escape him. When he reached the top, he halted, shifting sideways so that he came out to the left of the place where Vickers had fallen.

And saw the outlaw sprawled on the ground below.

Vickers still held the Colt, but he lay helpless and broken on the rocks ten feet down. When

Fisher reached him he tried to cock the gun. Fisher kicked it from his hand.

There was blood showing on Vickers' chest. More on his left shoulder. His right leg was twisted under him, broken. His face was a waxy yellow colour, sweat plastering the shiny black hair against his forehead. Only his eyes seemed alive, as burning bright as ever, the pale blue radiating hate at Fisher.

"You goddam bastard. I could've done it. Could've done it all. I might've won the war for the South."

"Sure," said Fisher, levelling the Navy Colt on the pale, spittle-flecked face. "Sure you could."

He pulled the trigger.

Jonas Vickers' face exploded in a messy welter of blood. Lee Fisher grunted as some of it splashed over his boots. Hell, he thought, that'll wash off. I hope the rest will, too.

He turned away, moving slowly through the darkness to his horse. The sun was all the way down now and lights were beginning to show in Skylar. He wondered if they were showing in Northville and Lawrence, and all the other bloody towns in Kansas, and the little cabins along the way.

For no particular reason he hoped they were.

THE END

DONOVAN
by Elmer Kelton

Donovan was supposed to be dead. The town had buried him years before when Uncle Joe Vickers had fired off both barrels of a shotgun into the vicious outlaw's face as he was escaping from jail. Now Uncle Joe had been shot—in just the same way.

CODE OF THE GUN
by Gordon D. Shirreffs

MacLean came riding home with saddle-tramp written all over him, but sewn in his shirt-lining was an Arizona Ranger's star. MacLean had his own personal score to settle—in blood and violence!

GAMBLER'S GUN LUCK
by Brett Austen

Gamblers hands are clean and quick with cards, guns and women. But their names are black, and they seldom live long. Parker was a hell of a gambler. It was his life—or his death . . .

ORPHAN'S PREFERRED
by Jim Miller

A boy in a hurry to be a man, Sean Callahan answers the call of the Pony Express. With a little help from his Uncle Jim and the Navy Colt .36, Sean fights Indians and outlaws to get the mail through.

DAY OF THE BUZZARD
by T. V. Olsen

All Val Penmark cared about was getting the men who killed his wife. All young Jason Drum cared about was getting back his family's life savings. He could not understand the ruthless kind of hate Penmark nursed in his guts.

THE MANHUNTER
by Gordon D. Shirreffs

Lee Kershaw knew that every Rurale in the territory was on the lookout for him. But the offer of $5,000 in gold to find five small pieces of leather was too good to turn down.

RIFLES ON THE RANGE
by Lee Floren

Doc Mike and the farmer stood there alone between Smith and Watson. Doc Mike knew what was coming. There was this moment of stillness, a clock-tick of eternity, and then the roar would start. And somebody would die . . .

HARTIGAN
by Marshall Grover

Hartigan had come to Cornerstone to die. He chose the time and the place, but he did not fight alone. Side by side with Nevada Jim, the territory's unofficial protector, they challenged the killers—and Main Street became a battlefield.

HARSH RECKONING
by Phil Ketchum

The minute Brand showed up at his ranch after being illegally jailed, people started shooting at him. But five years of keeping himself alive in a brutal prison had made him tough and careless about who he gunned down . . .

FIGHTING RAMROD
by Charles N. Heckelmann
Most men would have cut their losses, but Frazer counted the bullets in his guns and said he'd soak the range in blood before he'd give up another inch of what was his.

LONE GUN
by Eric Allen
Smoke Blackbird had been away too long. The Lequires had seized the Blackbird farm, forcing the Indians and settlers off, and no one seemed willing to fight! He had to fight alone.

THE THIRD RIDER
by Barry Cord
Mel Rawlins wasn't going to let anything stand in his way. His father was murdered, his two brothers gone. Now Mel rode for vengeance.

RIDE A LONE TRAIL
by Gordon D. Shirreffs
The valley was about to explode into open range war. All it needed was the fuse and Ken Macklin was it.

ARIZONA DRIFTERS
by W. C. Tuttle

When drifting Dutton and Lonnie Steelman decide to become partners they find that they have a common enemy in the formidable Thurston brothers.

TOMBSTONE
by Matt Braun

Wells Fargo paid Luke Starbuck to outgun the silver-thieving stagecoach gang at Tombstone. Before long Luke can see the only thing bearing fruit in this eldorado will be the gallows tree.

HIGH BORDER RIDERS
by Lee Floren

Buckshot McKee and Tortilla Joe cut the trail of a border tough who was running Mexican beef into Texas. They stopped the smuggler in his tracks.

HARD MAN WITH A GUN
by Charles N. Heckelmann

After Bob Keegan lost the girl he loved and the ranch he had sweated blood to build, he had nothing left but his guts and his guns but he figured that was enough.